"Nobody ever kisses you, Mom....

"I mean, except like me, like good-night, and that's not the same, not all gooey and stuff—the way Tim kissed you," Tuesday said, rolling her eyes at the folly of adults. She started to troop backward down the sidewalk, not waiting for her mother. "And that means he really likes you. So what I think is he likes you, you know, like a girlfriend, but you don't like him. And that's why you want him to go away."

"No, of course not. Tues, the main thing is that he just doesn't belong here."

Kally closed her eyes. This had to stop. She lived a controlled, orderly life, full of her daughter and her work and her schedules. Heated glances, a hard male body and warm, soft lips were not part of it.

She reached out and stroked her daughter's cheek. "I know you like him. And he likes you—"

"And he's a lot like a real daddy, Mom."

ABOUT THE AUTHOR

Julie Kistler loves combining screwball comedy with fantasy elements to come up with her very own special mix of humor and romance. She's been a solid contributor to the American Romance line for more than ten years, and her books continue to be reader favorites. Julie now lives in Illinois with her tall, dark and handsome husband, and their cat, Thisbe.

Books by Julie Kistler

HARLEQUIN AMERICAN ROMANCE

158—THE VAN RENN LEGACY
207—CHRISTMAS IN JULY
236—WILDFLOWER
266—ALWAYS A BRIDESMAID
329—BEST WISHES
418—CHRISTMAS IN TOYLAND
429—FLANNERY'S RAINBOW
471—FINN'S ANGEL
485—BLACK JACK BROGAN
511—CINDERELLA AT THE FIRECRACKER BALL
535—DREAM LOVER
557—ONCE UPON A HONEYMOON
575—RYAN'S BRIDE
593—FANTASY WIFE
690—TOUCH ME NOT

Tuesday's Knight

JULIE KISTLER

TORONTO • NEW YORK • LONDON
AMSTERDAM • PARIS • SYDNEY • HAMBURG
STOCKHOLM • ATHENS • TOKYO • MILAN • MADRID
PRAGUE • WARSAW • BUDAPEST • AUCKLAND

To my mom, Bertha Caplan Kistler,
so much a part of me always.

ISBN 0-373-16740-7

TUESDAY'S KNIGHT

This edition published by arrangement with Harlequin Books S.A.

Printed in U.S.A.

Chapter One

Nobody knew how long the mysterious bookshop had been there.

Tucked underneath a brownstone, it looked so old, so lonely, so curious that Kally had asked around about it. But even old Mrs. Libertini, who had been running the cleaner's on that block since before World War Two, said the bookshop predated her. Never busy, rarely open, it just sat there, the laziest store in Manhattan.

But it wasn't abandoned or anything. Of that Kally was certain. For one thing, the display in the front window changed regularly. Last month she'd noticed a dusty puppet theater taking center stage, and before that an ornate Victorian dollhouse.

Several times, as Kally had rushed past on her way to the subway, she had noticed a light inside the store. And once or twice, on her way to pick up her daughter after school, she'd seen a small white Open card in the front window, just under the faded gilt letters that spelled out Kew's Curiosity and Book Shop.

What did a curiosity shop carry, anyway? Kally couldn't help giving the shop a wistful glance. It was

Saturday, a gorgeous just-summer day, and early enough in the morning that the street didn't seem to have woken up yet. There was none of the customary hustle and bustle, no honking cabs, no double-parked trucks, not even a bicycle messenger. The florist next door had hosed part of the sidewalk, and the wet pavement reflected cool air at her. All in all, a lovely morning. Too nice to spend inside a dark little store.

Or at least that's what she told herself.

Gazing below the level of the sidewalk into its shadowy window, she could see the rosy glow of a pink lampshade, a big fluffy cat stretching next to a pretty gingerbread dollhouse, and behind it, in the depths of the store, she thought she saw something move. It gave her a strange tingle of anticipation. Yes, someone was definitely moving in there. Kally paused. The Open sign was posted. Should she…

"Look down there, Mommy!" her daughter said with excitement. Tuesday clasped the wrought-iron railing at street level, poking her small head partially through for a better view. "There's an awesome dollhouse in the window. And an even awesomer cat. Did you ever in your whole life see such a gigantosaurus cat?"

Tuesday was, as always, bubbling over with enthusiasm. She was a very smart little girl, much too old for her seven years, and she seemed to be in a hurry for everything.

"Look, Mommy," she said again, dancing with excess energy. "Did you see the kitty?"

"Yes, I saw it." Kally smiled fondly at her daughter. "But I thought you absolutely, positively had to get at least one teddy bear today or you would die."

"Oh, Mommy, we can look at bears any time. This is special."

Well, that was a surprise. Tuesday usually hung on for dear life when there was something she really wanted. And Kally had felt sure her daughter's desire for tiny teddy bears in pretty outfits wasn't going away.

Secretly, she was relieved. Designer bears were expensive, and Kally knew very well how far each dollar had to stretch these days. If only her ex-husband, Brad, the starving actor, would pay his child support remotely on time.

But that was Brad—always a day late and a dollar short.

"Look, Mommy! Did you see?" her daughter squealed. "The kitty is waving at me!"

"I don't really think it waved, Tuesday. Probably just stretched or something." But when she looked at the cat, it did appear to be gazing at Tuesday, lifting one white paw in the air and then curling it, as if beckoning to the little girl.

Kally blinked and looked again. It was licking its paw, like an ordinary cat doing an ordinary cat thing. Surely it hadn't...

"Mommy, I think the cat wants me to play with it."

"Well, maybe," Kally said doubtfully. "So do you want to go in? It might be nothing special, but who knows until we look?"

"I think we should definitely look inside," Tuesday

said in a serious tone. "Sometimes, Mommy, you just have to take a chance on things that look different."

Words to live by.

Kally led the way down the steps and carefully eased open the door. How odd to feel her pulse quicken, her nerves jump, as the bell over the door tinkled their arrival. What was it about Kew's Curiosity and Book Shop that made her feel so strange?

She scanned the place quickly, trying to make sure the store was an appropriate place for a seven-year-old before she let Tuesday in. But she saw a stand of old-fashioned paper-doll books straight ahead and a rack of papier-mâché masks behind that. A couple of the masks looked scary, but nothing that would bother Tuesday. Beyond those two special displays, books of every size and description spilled from shelves and cabinets.

Around the corner, a faded chintz armchair invited her to curl up with a book. It was centered on a small Persian rug, and a couple of big pillows and a pink fringed lamp made the scene even cozier.

Kally sent a glance at her daughter. All in all, it looked exactly like Tuesday's kind of place. A little odd, a little offbeat, in need of a vacuum and a dust mop, but overwhelmingly charming.

"Welcome," a small, musical voice announced. "I've been waiting for you."

"You have?" She looked around in vain for a body to go with the voice. "What do you mean?"

Behind her, Tuesday said hi in her brightest, cheeriest voice, pushing past her mother and striding in. As she did, a small man in a rich brocade and velvet jacket emerged from the shadows. His age was impossible to guess. He could've been anywhere from fifty to a hundred. He reminded Kally vaguely of someone, but it took her several seconds to pin it down.

Jiminy Cricket, she realized, glad she hadn't spoken her thought aloud. But there was something about the shape of his head and his bright little eyes that did remind her of a cartoon animal.

Meanwhile, Tuesday was giving him the once-over, her eyes wide with awe as she took in his impressive coat and funny velvet cap, which had a long tassel spilling over one side.

"Cool," she whispered. And then she asked, "Who are you?"

"It's not polite to ask that," Kally said quickly, but the man was beaming at her daughter as if he didn't mind at all.

"My name is Mr. Kew," he replied kindly. "I am the proprietor of Kew's Curiosity Shop. Please, come in." He swept out one arm to indicate the clutter of books around him. "We have many fascinating volumes which are sure to amuse you."

"Mr. Q?" Tuesday giggled. "Why does your name only have one letter?"

"No, honey, Kew, like on the outside of the store," Kally explained.

But Mr. Kew had a different explanation. "Perhaps my name indicates that I am a singular individual. Like your own, Tuesday."

Her daughter looked confused. But then the light dawned. "Does singular mean I'm the only one who's got it? I got called it because I was born on a Tuesday," she said importantly. "I never met another Tuesday, although there was once this Wednesday on TV. But she was weird."

Kally gave the store owner a small, uneven smile. "Yes, well, that's probably a little more than Mr. Kew needed to know, sweetie. Why don't you go look at the dollhouse? Or the cat. Remember the kitty who was waving at you?"

But as Tuesday ran off to inspect the cat, still curled up in the front window, Kally had another twinge, stronger this time. There was no other way to describe it—it was just a feeling, a warning, a momentary weirdness.

The old man knew her daughter's name. And she could swear she hadn't mentioned it.

"How did you..." she began, but he was no longer there.

Kally whirled. Mr. Kew was behind her, looking perfectly calm, wielding a rather large feather duster as he attended to a small table holding a few curios and a stack of leather-bound books.

"You said you were waiting for us. What did you mean?"

He shrugged. "You looked like people in need of a good book." Again, he swung out an arm, almost knocking over volumes ten through twelve of the complete history of the Peloponnesian wars, where they were piled carelessly on a nearby desk.

Kally moved quickly enough to catch the top volume on the stack before it hit the ground. "There," she said, sticking it back and steadying the whole pile. "Wouldn't want to lose the Peloponnesian wars."

"Mommy, Mommy," Tuesday said excitedly, running over with a whole lot of cat slung over one arm. "Dot likes me!"

"Dot?"

"It's her name," Tuesday declared.

Since her daughter was capable of naming and humanizing everything from house dust to Popsicle sticks, Kally thought she had this figured out. Unlike Mr. Kew's inexplicable knowledge of Tuesday's name, this name was made up. The cat was mostly black with big white spots, so Tues had named it Dot. "It's not polite to name other people's pets," she told her daughter, but she bent and petted the animal anyway. It blinked golden eyes at her and then purred loudly as she rubbed the top of its furry head.

"Oh, but Miss Tuesday is perfectly correct. Her name is Dot," Mr. Kew put in.

"But how did..." But then she saw the gold tag, shaped like a fish, jingling on the cat's collar. "Dot," she read aloud. "Aren't you clever, Tues, to read the tag?"

"Uh-huh. Here, Mommy, you hold the kitty while I look at the books, okay?" And without further ado, Tuesday lumped the huge cat into her mother's arms and raced down one of the narrow, book-lined aisles.

The cat was purring so loudly Kally couldn't put it down, although she did shout, "Tuesday, don't go far! Do you hear me? Stay where I can see you."

"I know, Mommy," her daughter yelled. She was

already perched on a stool, squinting to try to read the titles on the higher shelves.

And Mr. Kew was nowhere to be seen. He certainly did move quietly. Kally stood there, gingerly cradling the cat, picking up books with her free hand. Unfortunately, she must've ended up in the foreign language section. As she tried to decipher even a title, Tuesday came rocketing back.

"Mommy," she said, in an ominous tone that could mean anything from "I found a ladybug" to "I just flushed Grandma's dentures down the toilet."

"What's up?"

"Mommy, I found the *best* book." Tuesday grabbed her mother's hand and started to pull her down the aisle she'd come from. "It is totally cool."

Kally tried to divest herself of the cat, but it somehow managed to wind itself over her shoulder like a cape, so she just gave in and left it there. "And what is this fabulous book about?"

"Sir Lancelot and Arthur and Guinevere. Oh, Mom, it has pictures and everything!"

Kally sighed. She should've known. Other little girls wanted Disney videos or Barbie coloring books, but Tuesday wanted all these massive tomes on the Round Table. Ever since her grandmother took her to a matinee of the musical *Camelot* when she was five, she had been absolutely fascinated with anything and everything to do with King Arthur.

"I'm sure it is an amazing book, Tues, but you already have two books about King Arthur. Daddy gave you one for Christmas and Aunt Marena gave you another one for your birthday. Plus you have the Fantasy Adventures Castle *and* the Pretty, Pretty Princess Palace."

"I know. But this is different." Tuesday folded her arms over her bright pink T-shirt, fixing her mother with a feisty glare. She tried to pull a massive volume, almost as big as she was, from the floor. "Look, Mommy. You'll see."

With the cat still attached to her shoulder, Kally stooped to examine the book. It was impossibly thick, the binding was falling off, and the print was small enough to blind ordinary mortals. As she flipped the page, a cloud of dust arose, a moth flew out, and Kally sneezed loudly.

"Did you see the pictures?" her daughter asked hopefully.

Kally gave her a jaded eye but found a page with a picture just to fend off complaints later that she hadn't given the book a fair shot. It looked like a rather crude woodcut, prominently featuring a woman with very large breasts spilling from her clingy medieval dress, while the man next to her had muscles big enough for a cartoon hero. Meanwhile, some poor dragon was sitting there with a big sword through his tummy and blood spurting out. Even in black and white, it was horrific.

"Tues, this is really icky," she said, standing and brushing dust off her hands. "Your other books are much nicer. Besides, I don't think you can read print this small. And it looks like some sort of bug might've been living in the binding."

"I can so read it! I can read littler than that."

"I'm sure you can. But this isn't a good book for you."

"But Mommy," Tuesday said. But she hadn't even gotten to midargument when Mr. Kew popped up, just like that.

One minute there was nothing but a bookshelf behind her daughter, and the next, there was Mr. Kew, cocking his head, dangling his tassel in the air. "I have something I think is perfect for you," he said mysteriously. "Come with me, please."

The cat leaped, sprinting after its owner, while Kally and Tuesday had no choice but to bring up the rear. They wound down one aisle and up another, finally arriving where they'd started—at the front of the store. Mr. Kew had disappeared behind a counter, notable mostly for an ancient cash register and a wicker bird cage with a very large green parrot in it.

At first Kally thought maybe it was stuffed, but as they approached, it hopped up and down and let out a shriek. "Bawwwk. Hey, laaaaady. Hey, little girl, little girl. Bawwwwk. Have I got a book for you, boy-oh-boy!"

Tuesday hustled closer to her mother. With big eyes, she whispered, "Mommy, the bird talked to us."

"Be quiet, Henrik," the shop owner chided. "Don't make me cover your cage."

Kally kept her distance. It might be in a cage, but its beak was bigger than Tuesday's whole hand.

In a ripply little falsetto, the bird sang, "Everybody ought to have a book." Mr. Kew ignored it, reaching under the counter.

"Here it is," he said, his voice as twinkly as his

bright eyes. Confidentially, as if he didn't want the parrot to hear, he added, "I keep books for my special customers behind the desk."

"We're a special customer, Mommy," Tuesday echoed.

"Yes, I know." Kally was keeping her options open. She was waiting to see just what this special book would be. But her feelings of anticipation, of something unusual about to happen, were multiplying.

"One of a kind," Mr. Kew said, his voice ringing with reverence as he set the book before them. "*Sir Crispin, the Golden Knight of Yore.*"

Uh-oh. Once she heard the title, Kally knew Tuesday was a goner. And it *was* a beautiful book, no way around it.

It was oversize, but not nearly as massive as that hideous thing in the back of the store. And while it looked antique, it had been kept in perfect condition, with a robin's-egg blue cover and shiny gold lettering.

"It's cool," Tuesday breathed, touching it as if it were made of precious gems. She turned the cover, her eyes huge and sparkling, her mouth a round *O* of bliss. Right there, on the title page, Kally knew the battle was lost. The watercolor illustration—of a strong, brave knight in full armor and regalia, riding a golden steed—was so perfect, so mouthwateringly lovely, that Kally knew she had no hope whatsoever of wresting that book away from her daughter.

The print was even more exquisite, as if each letter had been hand-set and hand-inked by a master of the craft. The first letter on the first page—the *O* in "Once upon a time"—was grand and ornate, all swirling gilt and peacock blue, with tiny snakes and birds forming the letter. Exquisite.

"Come on, be brave," the parrot screeched. "I say, don't—don't be afraid."

"How much?" Kally couldn't bear that look of adoration in her daughter's eyes for one more minute if there was no way she could afford the book.

"Thirty dollars," said Mr. Kew. "Not very much, after all."

In Kally's tight budget, thirty dollars was a lot for a used book. But as her daughter turned the pages, as Kally took in the quality and care that had so obviously gone into every page, she couldn't refuse.

"I'll take it," she said with conviction, reaching for her wallet, and Tuesday turned and squeezed her and the book in one jubilant embrace.

Backing away, her daughter bubbled, "Mommy, Mommy, thank you, thank you! Hurry up and pay, okay? I want to go right home and read my whole book!"

"Right home? What about our other stops? What about the teddy bears?"

"We can see them some other time. Come on, Mom!"

This was truly extraordinary. Tuesday was willing to forget toys? Kally managed to say, "Okay, I'm coming."

At the last moment, she turned back. "Thank you, Mr. Kew. I'm sure Tuesday will love Sir Crispin."

"Ah, but he is for both of you." And then she could have sworn he winked at her from beneath his odd little hat. "A most magical book, Kally Malone. I hope it brings you both great pleasure."

What an odd thing to say, Kally thought. *And how did he know my name?*

But the only answer came from Henrik, the parrot.

"Come back soon to Kew's Curiosity Shop," it trilled loudly. "Where Curiosity is our middle name!"

Chapter Two

"Tuesday, this is the third time I've called you for dinner."

"But I'm just getting to the good part." Tuesday's eyes never left the page she was reading. "Sir Crispin's inside the castle of the Fair Rosaminda's father and he's in a contest to win her hand because her father already promised Rosaminda to the Dark Knight, and Sir Crispin can't let her go to the Dark Knight. Mommy, it's important! Sir Crispin can't let her get married to some other guy."

Kally fixed her daughter with a stern look, but Tuesday only bent closer, her long, honey brown hair falling to brush the page.

It was one thing for Tuesday to stay inside all afternoon on a beautiful day just so she could pore over every inch of *Sir Crispin, the Golden Knight of Yore.* But it was quite another to disobey and talk back when it was time to come to the table. Tuesday knew better than that.

Every night, they had the same routine. It had been that way since before the divorce, even back in the old days when Brad could never be counted on to show up. He always had some half-baked audition to go to, some new agent or producer to try to get in to see. But husband or no husband, Kally had decided that her child would have a set schedule and a classic family-around-the-table dinner every night.

Okay, so the family had turned out to be just the two of them. They had no homey country kitchen, no charming dining room—just a minuscule nook off the living room of their tiny apartment. And their nightly fare tended to be pizza and French fries. It didn't matter. What was really important was that they were together.

So far, Kally had made good on her promise to keep dinner special. And she didn't plan to stop just because Tuesday was swept away in some fantasy world of knights and damsels in distress.

"Tuesday," she repeated. "Now."

The dire tone at least got the child to pull her eyes away from the page. "Please, Mommy," she whined. "Can't I read just a few more minutes?"

Kally crossed her arms over her chest. "Let me put it this way. Either you put the book away now and come set the table, or the next time you see Sir Crispin you'll be old enough to vote."

Still the book lay open on her lap. Kally could tell Tuesday was hesitating, reluctant to set it aside, her eyes dreamy as her small finger traced one of the illustrations.

What *was* it about that book?

Sure, the pictures were pretty, but Tuesday was acting as if she were in a trance. Giving up a chance at bean-bag bears, ignoring candy and snacks, refusing to take phone calls from two different little friends and now paying no attention to dinner.

"The other book had a moth in it. Maybe this one came with a hypnotist," she said under her breath. But Tuesday wasn't listening.

Kally suddenly foresaw the battle she was going to have at bedtime, and she decided she was going to nip this in the bud right now.

"Okay," she said, in a very no-nonsense sort of voice, advancing on her daughter. "Time's up, kiddo."

Before Tuesday had time to figure out what was going on, Kally reached down and nabbed the book. A wail arose from her child's lips, but Kally remained firm. With the object of contention firmly under one arm, she swept over to the tiny kitchen, reached up and shoved *Sir Crispin* behind the bowls in the highest cupboard. It fell into a space at the back with a satisfying thud.

"Mommy," Tuesday wailed. "Give it back!"

Kally refused to budge.

"But Mommy," her daughter said, doing her best to look pitiful. "I need to finish my story. Sir Crispin was just tricking the Dark Knight to get in a bag and then he's going to thump him."

"That doesn't sound very heroic. Besides, you can look at it again tomorrow."

Tuesday's mouth opened, but Kally held her off.

"Tomorrow."

Wordlessly, she handed over plates and silverware.

She could hear muttering and griping as Tuesday marched her little self over to slap down the place settings. Specific words were hard to pick out, but Kally got the idea well enough. Mean mother, poor, put-upon child, unfairly dragged away from the best and most wonderful book ever written.

Then Tuesday spent the entire meal sulking, at least when she wasn't gazing at the cupboard with longing eyes. Kally could almost see the calculations going on in her daughter's eyes. *Let's see, if I open the refrigerator and climb to the top shelf, and then lean over far enough to catch the edge of the cabinet door...*

"Don't even think about it," Kally said evenly. "As soon as you go to bed, I'm moving it."

"Mommy, you can't!"

"Eat your peas." She hated behaving like a mean mom more than Tuesday hated living with one, but there was no choice. Not when Tues was acting like this. It was so unlike her. But if she was this stubborn when she was seven, what was she going to be doing at thirteen? Kally didn't even want to think about it.

It was a very long evening. After dinner, Kally pulled out a puzzle she and Tuesday had been putting together for weeks, one tiny piece at a time, but her daughter just looked the other way and chewed on the ends of one long tendril of her hair.

The evening didn't get any shorter when Brad called and Tuesday ran to speak to him as if he were, well, Sir Crispin, the Golden Knight. And then she complained in long, impassioned detail about how unreasonable Mommy was and would Daddy please, please, please come and rescue her?

Kally did her best to ignore it.

The phone conversation lagged on for some time,

and when it was finally over, Tuesday listlessly lumped herself in front of the television.

Kally could no longer stand the tension. "I'm sorry, but you were just too attached to that book. You'd been reading for five or six hours straight."

"Wanted to finish."

"You can finish tomorrow." Kally paused, wondering how much of her daughter's phone conversation she should poke into. "What did Daddy have to say?"

"Got a new job."

"Well, that's good." She had no illusions about her ex-husband's exciting acting career, however. Brad's jobs never amounted to more than a few hours as a fast-food chicken or maybe a nonspeaking part as a tap-dancing tomato. His big break thus far had been playing a corpse in an episode of a New York-based cop show.

Tuesday volunteered, "He's in a cold commercial."

"A cold commercial?"

"Uh-huh. I think he said he plays a drippy nose, like when you have a cold. He said the costume is really awesome, like, a three-foot nostril or something." Her daughter showed the first animation she'd had all night, while Kally tried not to snicker. "And he has a thing in his hand that he squeezes to make the big nose run with slimy green stuff. Isn't that cool?"

"Totally. And he's graduated to body parts. How nice." She hoped Tuesday wasn't quite old enough to appreciate sarcasm.

But there wasn't time to worry. Just then the floor began vibrating and trembling.

"Sounds like Rosie is working on a new routine," Kally said. Their next-door neighbor was a bouncy blond aerobics instructor who spent every waking moment either at the gym or practicing for the gym. Kally and Tuesday usually enjoyed trying to guess what the music was from thc tcmpo of Rosie's jumps and thumps. "What do you think? *Star Wars* again?"

But tonight Tuesday just shrugged and gave her mother a grumpy glance, refusing to be captured by the usual games.

The fifth floor's noise level suddenly went up another notch, as angry footsteps clomped up the stairs and down the hall. The monster footfalls were joined by the knock of a meaty fist against wood. *Boom. Boom. Boom.* The knocks reverberated so loudly it sounded as if Kally's door was the one getting assaulted.

Wait a minute—that *was* her door.

She put aside the puzzle piece she was holding and went to the door, peeking through the little hole for the sake of security, but she already knew who it would be. Mrs. Krasselbine. Eagle-eyed, eagle-eared Mrs. Krasselbine, always on the lookout for violations. Her son owned the building, and she was constantly threatening to get people evicted if they broke the rules. Just Kally's luck that the evil Mrs. K lived right underneath *her* apartment. But this time, Kally knew she was clean.

"Hello, Mrs. Krasselbine," she said sweetly, unhooking the chain and clicking the dead bolt. "What can I do for you?"

"What is that racket?" The old woman had brought a sturdy cane with her, and she pounded it into Kally's threshold to emphasize her words.

Less than five feet tall, weighing no more than a hundred pounds, she was still a force to be reckoned with. Especially when she was quivering with rage and indignation—like right now. She had scraped her steely gray hair into a bun and then speared a pair of chopsticks through it. Even the chopsticks were quivering.

"Have you got a pack of wild horses in there or what? I swear, my ceiling is going to be coming down in chunks!"

"Not us." Kally swung the door open wider to give Mrs. K a better look inside. She decided Old Eagle Ears must be getting deaf if she couldn't tell where the noise was coming from. It was so obviously streaming out from under Rosie's door.

Except that the din cut off abruptly. Rosie was taking a break.

Mrs. K's unpleasant face got even more unpleasant. "Ha! Well, you're clever, aren't you? Stopping just when you heard me coming. But I tell you, I know you've got gypsies in there."

"Gypsies?"

"Or gymnasts maybe." Mrs. Krasselbine squinted for a better look. "Having a party, were you?"

"Not doing a darn thing." Kally moved to close the door. "Now, if you'll excuse us—"

"All right, I suppose you win. This time. But just

because I'm an old woman don't think you can pull the wool over my eyes!''

''Never, Mrs. Krasselbine.''

As soon as the cranky old lady was gone, Kally bolted her door and sighed with relief. The last thing she needed was to be evicted, even from this tiny, less-than-swanky place.

''Tues, it's time for bed,'' she called, thankful that it really was finally that time. What with her daughter's case of the sulks, her ex's new job as a nostril, Rosie's disco inferno and Mrs. Krasselbine's snooping, this evening had already gone on much too long.

With a few last mournful glances at the kitchen cupboard, Tuesday consented to brush her teeth and finally, blessedly, bunk down. She even let her mother tuck her in, sort of.

As Kally switched off the light, her daughter whispered, ''Mom, you said tomorrow I could have Sir Crispin back, right?''

''You really have a one-track mind, you know that?''

She closed Tuesday's door, shaking her head. But at least it reminded her to get the book out of the cupboard and put it somewhere else before she turned in. She could just imagine Tuesday, barefoot and in her jammies, tiptoeing into the dark kitchen at four o'clock to rescue her beloved volume. She'd be crashing over chairs and clattering dishes to try to stand in the sink. And then what would Mrs. Krasselbine say?

Kally smiled at the very idea.

She couldn't quite reach the thing herself, and she ended up having to pull over a chair to climb high enough to retrieve *Sir Crispin, the Golden Knight of Yore.*

"Wonder why she's so attached to this," she mused, giving the front cover a casual glance.

How funny that the apartment was a little stuffy tonight, but Sir Crispin's binding felt cool to the touch. Kally ran her fingers over the embossed letters. The cover was a lovely shade of blue, with a gold-embossed title. Her index finger seemed to tremble, to tingle, when she traced the shiny foil letters.

"Maybe I should take a look," she whispered. After all, it wasn't her bedtime yet. And if she left it until Tuesday was awake, she'd never see Sir Crispin again.

After clicking off the kitchen light, Kally padded into the living room. She was going to curl up on the couch with the oversize volume, but at the last moment, she decided to be comfortable. So she made up the sofa bed where she slept, pulled on a favorite nightshirt and settled in.

And then she opened *Sir Crispin, the Golden Knight of Yore.* There was that tingle again, only stronger. With a deep breath, she flipped to the first page.

Before she knew it, she was knee-deep in chivalrous adventures as virile, courageous Sir Crispin continued to try to foil his nemesis, the Dark Knight.

Once upon a time, in a land of shimmering green dingles and gossamer dales, where dragons breathed fire and captive princesses tarried behind tall towers, there lived two knights.

One was as golden as the other was dark, as opposite as night and day.

As chance and fate conspired to play their wicked

games, the two boys were born on the very same misty morning in May, separated only by the wide dark Lake of Midnight.

There was much rejoicing and joy in the Golden Vale of Glinn, where the birth of the gilt-haired, blue-eyed son was much anticipated.

But in the cold castle of the Lord of Midnight, there was no such merriment. Seventh son, lean and dark, with eyes as deep and forbidding as the Lake of Midnight itself, this boy was no one's favorite.

And as their fortunes swept them hither and yon, the golden boy, Sir Crispin as he was called, grew up strong and true, brave and brash, lusty and hale…

"Strong, brave and true," Kally repeated. "Wow. What I wouldn't give for a knight in shining armor to walk into *my* life."

She read on. *But the Dark Knight, overlooked and unloved, came to manhood fierce and moody, silent and resolute, his sword as skillful as his rival, but his heart as black as night…*

She soaked up the words eagerly, scanning page after page, drinking in the glorious illustrations. Whoever the artist was, he'd done some fabulous work on this one. The words detailing Sir Crispin's feats flew past, but the pictures swirled around her, fascinating her, catching her. Why, she could almost breathe his air, as if Sir Crispin's golden, manly scent filled her nose, as if his crystal blue eyes blazed off the page, searching just for her.

Every inch of Sir Crispin's finely hewn body seemed to burst with life and vigor. His tawny tresses streamed out behind him, curling over the shiny, smooth surface of his golden armor.

"He's beautiful," she whispered.

Drowsily, Kally traced one finger along the bulging line of his thigh, the throbbing curve of one bicep, the long, cold angle of his sword. How could a picture in a child's book seem so alive?

On every page, lurking somewhere in the shadows, the Dark Knight provided stark contrast. His armor was etched in inky hues, and he carried a dark red shield that showed seven coal black, soaring birds. Kally shivered. Sir Crispin's golden beauty was lovely, but the Dark Knight's malevolent power was every bit as strong, every bit as potent.

Her eyes were growing heavy, and she knew she was falling asleep where she lay, still holding the book. But, like Tuesday before her, she couldn't let it go. "I just need to read a few more pages," she murmured, blinking to stay awake, to read on and find out what happened when Sir Crispin dipped his sword in the magic Fountain of Evermore and then scaled the walls of the Fair Rosaminda's castle.

With visions of mighty steeds and flashing blades whirling and spinning through her mind, Kally's eyes drifted shut, the book slipped from her hands, and finally, sweetly, she sank into a misty, dream-filled sleep.

"Sir Crispin," she whispered, snuggling into her pillow. "Mmm... Dark Knight..."

Deep in her dreams, he rode along a shadowy forest trail, his sword aloft, his sinewy thighs wrapped around the flanks of a proud stallion. She heard the furious hoofbeats and she stopped, paralyzed with fear and longing. And then he pulled alongside her, reaching for her, and she had no choice but to be swept up in his powerful arms…

When the most appalling racket came crashing through her dream.

Groggy, Kally sat up in bed. "Tuesday? Is that you?"

But it wasn't Tuesday.

Kally choked. She cowered in her bedclothes. Surely she was still dreaming.

Because there were two full-grown men fighting in her living room.

And they were wearing armor.

"What the—" Kally's voice sounded quavery and funny even to her own ears. She pinched herself. "Yeow. Oh, no. I'm awake!"

And if she was awake, that meant there were knights. With swords. Inches from her bed.

One's armor was shiny gold while the other wore darker silver, etched in black. A big, sky blue plume danced on top of the gold one's helmet, zigging and zagging every which way as he tromped around the dim room. Armor? Plumes?

Kally raised a shaky hand to her forehead.

But the two men fought on, as fiercely as if their lives depended upon it, crashing their swords and bashing each other and generally making a mess of her living room.

"There can't be knights in my living room!" she wailed.

But there were. The bigger one, the gold one,

slashed with his sword, and his opponent, the dark one, leaped straight into the air to avoid being skewered. Even in her current frame of mind, Kally realized that was pretty fancy footwork.

Of course, he came within an inch of taking out her television set when he did it, so maybe admiration wasn't the right choice.

"This is insane," she whispered.

"Mommy, why are those guys fighting in our apartment?" Tuesday asked, leaning over the back of the sofa. "Don't you think they're kind of loud? What if they wake up Mrs. Krasselbine?"

Oh, no. Tuesday saw it, too. Were there such things as group hallucinations?

Kally reached behind the sofa and stuffed her daughter into a crouch. "Stay there."

She threw a pillow and a couple of couch cushions over the back for further protection. Just as she did, the gold guy's sword came slicing through the mattress of her sofa bed, mere inches from her bare foot.

"Stop that!" She leaped to a standing position, clutching the comforter to her for protection. "Who do you think you are?"

But, like most men in the thrall of a good fight, they paid no attention. As she watched, horrified, the big gold knight hammered his smaller, leaner opponent, bashing him on the shoulder and then full against the side of his helmet. The apartment echoed with the clatter of metal against metal. Kally winced. The poor thing. His ears would be ringing for weeks.

With one mighty boot and the point of his sword firmly pinning the other knight to the edge of the sofa bed, the victor turned the pointy part of his golden helmet her way. His voice rang out through a layer of gold when he asked, quite politely, "Shall I deliver the death blow, my lady?"

Kally had enough presence of mind to cry, "No!" Quickly, she amended, "I mean, let him go. And get out of my apartment, both of you!"

Meanwhile, Tuesday had popped up from behind the couch, her eyes wide as saucers. Kally was scared witless, and her daughter was grinning from ear to ear. "This is way cool, Mommy."

Kally pushed her under the pillows.

"My lady," the broad-shouldered knight in the golden armor said again. And then he shoved up his visor and smiled at her.

She gulped for air. Her heart turned over.

Because he was stunning. Not just stunning, but absolutely, bigger-than-life, over-the-top gorgeous, with clear, aqua-blue eyes, a classic square jaw and finely sculpted lips.

Just peeking over the couch, Tuesday let out an audible gasp. "It's Sir Crispin!" she yelped.

"Of course it's not." No matter how much this guy looked like Sir Crispin, he was *not* Sir Crispin. Of course not.

"Is so," Tuesday said stubbornly.

"Maybe they're actors," Kally tried. "From Medieval Land or something. Remember when Daddy worked there? Your father must've sent them as a joke." She laughed, but it sounded phony even to her. "Some joke."

"I give you my solemn word, as a knight of the

realm, that this is no jest, m'lady," the Golden Knight declared in a strong, ringing voice. "And, as a sign of my vow to respect and honor every fair flower of womanhood I encounter upon my journey, I will release the Dark Knight, as you have requested."

Bowing his helmeted head, swishing his bright blue plume to and fro, he heaved himself backward, removing his massive foot and even bigger sword from the smaller knight's armored throat.

"Your daddy made it a very good joke," Kally managed to say around the panic clogging her throat.

"No, Mommy," Tuesday persisted. "This *is* Sir Crispin."

"Indeed I am that knight errant." Sweeping off his helmet, he shook free his golden curls. They tumbled down his back, curving around the cold metal of his gilded shoulder plates, just like in the book.

Kally gulped. Was she completely losing it? This just couldn't be.

"Yes, m'lady, it is I, Sir Crispin, known throughout the kingdom for derring-do, for the triumph of virtue over evil."

With a flourish, he bent on one creaky metal knee, barely missing the coffee table and a lamp as he swung his sword to salute her.

"Your servant, my lady," he said grandly.

Kally took a good look at the knocked-over table and crushed lamp, at the deep slash in the mattress, at the gorgeous, broad-shouldered knight, complete with shining armor, who was beaming at her from in front of her coffee table.

It couldn't be. But it was.

Sir Crispin, the Golden Knight of Yore, had walked off the pages of a book.

And into her living room.

Chapter Three

"There has to be some rational explanation," she said weakly. "Something that makes sense. Like a practical joke. Or burglars. Burglars hopped up on dungeon games."

"No, no, no," Tuesday insisted, grabbing her sleeve. "They came out of the book. Really, honestly, truly. Like magic. Like Merlin. Because how else did they get here? They sure didn't come in the door."

Trust her daughter to go right to the heart of things. A glance at the door told her it was still locked and bolted. And there was no way these guys had scaled five floors straight up the outside of her building in full armor.

No broken windows. No splintered locks.

How did they get here?

"W-who sent you?" she asked bravely. "Tell me how you got here. Tell me right now!"

"Indeed, I have no answer, m'lady," Sir Crispin said with an air of confusion. "I last remember casting my lance on the field of honor at the festival of King Issinglass. The day was excellent fine, and a golden bird swooped right down upon the field. I took it for a good omen—that my sword and I would cut a mighty path through the finest knights in the land and do honor to the colors of the Fair Rosaminda. Indeed, I bested one knight after the other until only the Dark Knight remained.'' His eyes narrowed. ''I beg pardon for uttering the name of so base a foe in a lady's presence.''

He shook his head, sending his tousled curls into a tailspin of careless beauty. Almost against her will, Kally watched the tendrils frolic over his breastplate. Fabulous. She had never seen a man with such gorgeous hair. It made her want to touch it, run her fingers through…

Oh, no. She refused to go there. No lustful feelings for a figment of her imagination. Trying to hold onto some semblance of sanity, she grabbed her protective comforter closer. ''Cut the speeches, buster. I want an explanation, and I want it now.''

But Sir Crispin only shrugged his massive shoulders. ''I have none, my lady.''

If he wasn't going to tell her voluntarily, what could she do? Torture him? *He* was the one with the deadly weapon.

From behind Kally, a darker, more dangerous voice growled, ''Who are you? What is this place?''

Kally whirled. The Dark Knight. Standing there all gaga over Sir Crispin's golden beauty, she'd forgotten about the other one. Although he had not removed his helmet, she could feel the intensity of his dark gaze, hear the flinty edge in his voice.

''Quickly now, wench. I've no time for games. Who are you?''

His tone sent shivers down her spine. Still, she didn't take that kind of insult from anyone, not even from the scariest villain in Christendom. "Wench? Just who do you think you're calling a wench, mister?"

His visor swung to focus on Tuesday. "Young princess, will you answer me?"

She smiled, waving a small hand in greeting. "Princess? Cool! I'm Tuesday. Princess Tuesday."

"Stop that," Kally instructed her. But it was too late.

"And this," Tuesday continued, pointing to her mother, "is Kally. Short for Kallista, but nobody ever calls her that."

The Dark Knight moved closer to the child. "What is this place, princess? Where are we?"

"It's an apartment," Tuesday said helpfully, moving a bit closer and gesturing out the window. "In New York City. You can see stuff out there, kind of, although mostly you can just see bricks from the building next door."

"The city of York is familiar to me," he mused. "Of *New* York I have not heard."

"York! A cold and unpleasant place." Sir Crispin sniffed. "Why anyone should desire a new one is beyond me. I do not think I like this *New* York any better than the old one."

Her head whirling, Kally eased off the bed to a place where she could keep an eye on both of them. Crispin stood very still, his shiny helmet in his hand, steadily flashing those pearly whites. Was it her imagination, or was he admiring his reflection in the surface of his headgear?

On the other side of the couch, the Dark Knight scanned the surroundings, turning the front of his visor this way and that. "We are presently inside a fortified tower, I can see that. How came you to be here, little princess?" he inquired, directing his attention to Tuesday. "Is this the castle of your father?"

"Um, no." Tuesday glanced at her mother for direction. "My dad hasn't lived here since I was really little. Um, I guess, well, it's kind of Mrs. Krasselbine's son's castle, is that right, Mommy?"

"You are the mother of the young princess?" His visor swung her way. "Ah. Beg pardon, Lady Kallista. I took you to be her handmaiden."

"Handmaiden?" This was going too far. In the book, knights were brave and wonderful. But here, in her living room, one of them was stuck on his own reflection while the other was full of insults. "Wench. Handmaiden. What next?"

Not that it mattered. It was all a crazy dream, and as soon as she got a grip or woke up or something, they would go away. Sir Crispin would take his blond good looks, and the Dark Knight would take his surly attitude, and the two of them would vanish into thin air.

It was going to happen any minute now. She was sure of it.

But in the meantime… What should she do?

While she considered the options, she knew one thing for sure. She didn't trust either of these guys, not even in shining armor. If they really were knights somehow tossed upon her shores like flotsam after a shipwreck, they would no doubt come complete with some code of honor. Chivalry and all that. But their code of what was right wouldn't necessarily accord with *her* code of what was right. So far, they had demonstrated that they certainly didn't know how to behave in a fifth-floor apartment.

On the other hand, if they weren't the real Sir Crispin and the Dark Knight, then who were they? Maybe actors or thieves, sent by strange little Mr. Kew to scam the people who bought the book? Okay, so it was a long shot. But what else made sense?

Kally raised a hand to her forehead. She could still hear that goofy parrot. *Kew's Curiosity Shop, where Curiosity is our middle name..*

Shaking her head, she muttered, "None of this makes sense."

Meanwhile, Tuesday was standing on her tiptoes to try to peer through the slits on the Dark Knight's helmet. "So, Mr. Dark Knight, sir," she said cheerfully, "how come you don't get a girl of your own and you let Sir Crispin have the Fair Rosaminda? You seem really nice and everything."

"Tuesday, stop talking to that...knight," Kally ordered, edging over far enough to catch her daughter and pull her to safety. "You know you're supposed to stay away from strangers."

"But, Mommy, he's not a stranger," her daughter protested. "He's the Dark Knight. He's even got the shield and everything, with seven black hawks on a red background."

"In the proper parlance, my arms are seven hawks sable on a field of gules," the Dark Knight told her.

"Oh, yeah," Tuesday said. "I forgot about that, how they have their own words for the colors. Anyway, he's got seven hawks because he's the seventh son, and they're black, um, sable, because his dad is that lord, you know. Oh, shoot. I forgot his name. The lord as black as midnight?"

"The Lake of Midnight," he amended. "I am the seventh son of the Lord of the Lake of Midnight."

Kally didn't know whether to be more astounded that he was such a stickler for the proper form or that he could say things like "the seventh son of the Lord of the Lake of Midnight" with a straight face.

"This is some kind of joke, right?"

The Dark Knight drew himself up to his full height. Although not as impressive as the majestic Sir Crispin, he was still quite imposing, especially covered in steel. And especially when he was front and center in such a small apartment. All he had to do was swing one battle-ready arm, and he could break a window, knock down an end table and dent the refrigerator.

"A jest, m'lady? I fail to see anything humorous in our present predicament."

"Well, I don't think it's too funny, either. And you know, the least you can do is take off your helmet," Kally said suddenly. "It's very hard to talk to someone when you can't see his face."

She hadn't a clue where that came from. Until this moment, she hadn't worried one bit about his hat. But all of a sudden, she didn't like wondering what was going on inside that tin can.

There was silence for a moment. Tension crackled in the air.

"Of course I would endeavor to remove my helm in the presence of a lady. I attempted to do so some moments ago. But I fear it is most grievously wedged. My colleague, Sir Rash-and-Reckless there, landed a cowardly blow, which seems to have dented me sufficiently to allow no egress."

He cuffed one gauntleted hand against the side of his head to demonstrate.

"Cowardly? Forbear from such slanders, sirrah, or you shall taste the blade of my weapon once more!" thundered Sir Crispin, waving his sword in the air.

"Could we all calm down, please?" Kally moved delicately between them, keeping Tuesday safely behind her. Something had to be done to keep these overgrown schoolboys from getting into another fight. So she stepped into mom mode. "First of all, both of you pipe down."

"Pipe down?" they chorused.

The Dark Knight added, "What means this?"

"It means you should be quiet," Kally snapped. "Tuesday, sweetheart, I need you to please go over there and sit down—as far away as possible from the knights—and stop jumping around. You," she said to Sir Rash-and-Reckless, still brandishing his sword, "put that thing down. And you—" she turned to the Dark Knight "—quit insulting everyone."

"Beg pardon, m'lady," he said in a surly tone that belied his apology.

He tipped his head, and Kally held her breath, hoping he wouldn't topple over completely, throwing himself off-balance like that. But he righted himself with a jerk and a muffled oath.

"Are you okay?" She edged over to see what the problem was with his helmet. One glance told the story. There was a little rivet that fitted into a small slot on the side, and it was badly bent, enough to keep the visor from opening. "You know, it looks like you should be able to get out of this."

So close, staring at him, she could just make out his eyes in there, and she could tell that they were very dark, darker than bittersweet chocolate, with thick, black lashes. Not the crystalline blue of his fellow knight, but very deep and very compelling. Right now, those eyes were shooting sparks at her, sparks of temper and frustration.

"I hesitate to press you, m'lady, but it is infernal hot inside here. If you could manage..."

She could definitely feel the heat he was talking about. She backed up a step. "I'm, uh, fairly sure we can at least pry your little door open so you can breathe." Backing up rapidly, she moved into the kitchen and started to rummage under the sink. "I thought I had some WD-40. And maybe a screwdriver."

"Mommy, Mommy, I figured it out," Tuesday said suddenly, leaping out of her chair and hopping on one foot.

"Sweetheart, Mommy is really busy right now." Kally frantically examined one label after another while the two knights cooled their jets, making "grrr" noises at each other.

"But, Mommy, I really think I've got it!"

"In a minute, Tues." Kally whirled, carrying a tub of margarine, a pair of pliers and a can opener. "Sir Crispin, really! I told you to put that sword in its holster."

"Refer you to my scabbard, m'lady?" he asked incredulously. He staggered where he stood. "Methinks we are in some enchanted land, where pipes are not for blowing but for downing, where a man's sword goes not in his scabbard but in his kolster. What is this New York?"

"Um, that was *holster,*" Tuesday said politely. "A coaster is what you put your cup on so it doesn't make a ring on the coffee table. If you guys are going to get along here, you need to learn stuff like that. Otherwise, people will think you're weird. 'Course, there's lots of weird people here, so maybe no one will notice."

"Stand still," Kally ordered the Dark Knight. She worked on greasing up his rivet. "Tuesday, honey, they don't need to get along, because they're not staying. They're just…a hallucination. I'm sure they'll be leaving—poof—any minute."

"Oh, Mommy," her daughter said pityingly. "Why would they come all this way from the book, like a magic spell and everything, just to go poof?"

"Sweetie, we don't know where they came from—"

"Of course we do. From the book. I was trying to tell you, Mommy, because I really, really, really think I got it figured out." Tuesday's eyes danced, and her little heart-shaped face was alive with anticipation. "It's just cool, cool, cool."

"Okay, in a minute, sweetheart." By holding onto

the pliers and pulling with all her might, Kally got the rivet to slide across. And then she used the can opener to pry the other fasteners off. She was not the most mechanical person on the face of the earth, and she thought this was pretty much a miracle.

Pulling away that small metal door, she found herself very curious to see just who would emerge.

Framed in steel, she saw a lean, saturnine face, dark brows, sharply angled cheekbones and a very ferocious expression. Not at all like Crispin's big, handsome, open face. Not at all.

Kally swallowed. She took a step back. "Uh, you can come out now."

"Could you pull off my gauntlet, if you please?" He held out his left hand. "I require the use of a hand to remove my helm."

Why was she feeling so strange about touching him? He was covered in layers of fabric and steel, for heaven's sake. Nothing to be afraid of. Gathering her courage, she drew his steel-covered hand into hers to unbuckle his glove and pull it off. It reminded her of the collapsible cup she'd had as a Girl Scout way back when. But she never would've thought of wearing a collapsible cup on her hand. "How do you do this at home?"

"Why, my squire arms me, of course," he answered. He arched an eyebrow. "Have you never heard of a squire, my lady?"

"I think so. Squire Tuck and Robin Hood?" She glanced at Tuesday for confirmation, but her daughter heaved a big sigh of disgust.

"Mother! That's *Friar* Tuck. He's bald and wears

a big old brown dress. Squire is something else. Like a helper, a kid who grows up to be a knight."

"Okay, okay." Gingerly, Kally laid the big glove on the sofa. Separate like that, it wasn't very attractive. Very Dr. Strangelove. When she turned, she saw that the Dark Knight had used his left hand to undo his helmet—there were apparently straps of some sort inside—and he grunted as he carefully maneuvered it off.

He gazed at her, and she gazed right back.

His eyes seemed to blaze with pride and honor, as if he knew exactly who he was and defied anyone to find him wanting. His hair was long, not quite black, instead a warm mahogany, a shade or two darker than Kally's. A bit tangled, a bit wild, it hung past his shoulders, as uncompromising as the rest of him, and it framed his fine features beautifully.

"Well," was all she could manage to say.

Tuesday covered it for both of them. "Hey, Mr. Dark Knight, you're pretty! They never showed your face in the book."

"Ahem," said Sir Crispin. "If you are all finished playing nursemaid to my pitiful opponent, could we perhaps return to our discussion? What is this place, this New York? And what mission must I accomplish to satisfy the code of chivalry? I am sworn, as a knight of the Round Table, never to shrink from any adventure, no matter how daring, and always to take up arms to defend the weak and persecuted." He scanned Kally's form. "Are you weak? Are you persecuted?"

"See? That's what I was trying to tell you," Tuesday chimed in. "Why they're here and all—they're on a quest, Mommy. Like to find some Holy Grail or something. Right here in our apartment. Isn't it fabuloso?''

''We don't have any Holy Grails.''

''Maybe we do and we don't know it,'' her daughter said logically. ''We have some cool cups. Maybe one of them is in disguise. Or under a spell.''

Kally found a smile for her daughter. ''That's very sweet, honey, and I know you're trying to help. But I really don't think your Little Mermaid toothbrush cup is going to turn into a Holy Grail just because you want it to.''

''But I wanted to see Sir Crispin for real, and he got here, didn't he?''

Of course, Kally had also made a small wish for a knight in shining armor, but she preferred not to think about that. ''Tuesday, you don't just make a wish and get guys from books to show up. Things like that don't happen, not in real life.''

Tuesday crossed her arms and tossed her hair. ''So how else did they get here?''

''The young princess makes a fair amount of sense,'' the Dark Knight announced grimly. ''A quest, indeed. But not to search out any holy relic. No, it is apparent to me that a wicked enchantment is at work here.''

''What?'' Kally wasn't at all sure what that was supposed to mean. Whose wicked enchantment? Did he think she and Tuesday were practicing sorcery on the side? ''First you think I'm a wench and now a witch. This is getting worse and worse.''

''Oh, no, Lady Kallista, do not mistake me. I do not

suggest that you and the young princess are sorceresses. On the contrary, I feel sure that you and your daughter are the victims of an evil wizard. There are signs of it everywhere." His piercing gaze swept her. "From your speech and manner I can surmise that you are highborn, yet you wear rags."

Kally looked at her baggy nightshirt. It was a well-worn New York Jets jersey, its letters faded, with a stain near the neck from eating chocolate ice cream in bed. It also wasn't the greatest cover in the world, especially without the quilt she'd been clutching earlier. Her cheeks flamed as she realized she'd been running around that way for some time.

Oh, dear. So that was why he thought she was a wench. Quickly, she grabbed the coverlet off the floor and gathered it around her.

But his terse voice continued. "And your hair is quite shamefully shorn."

"Shorn?" Kally liked her hair this way. It was a short, wispy shag, and she'd gotten it cut this way when she was feeling quite—well, spunky. It was a little disheveled right now, but when she had time to blow it dry and style it, it was really cute. Not fancy or anything, but cute. "You mean women can't have short hair where you're from? What about Joan of Arc? What's so shameful about *her* short hair?"

"I am not acquainted with your Joan of Arc. But it makes no matter." He eyed the room. "Of import is the fact that you are being held captive in this tower. Consider that Sir Crispin and I were whisked here as if by some otherworldly force, that strange words tumble from your mouths, words that bespeak enchantment." He added slowly, "I feel there can be no doubt. And I have been brought here to break the spell."

"A wicked spell! Way cool!" Tuesday cried, clapping her hands.

"You were brought here to break the spell? Clearly *I* am the one called upon to be the spell breaker!" Sir Crispin boomed, grasping his sword. "I, after all, roam the countryside performing good deeds, whereas you are a knave and an evildoer. Everyone knows of the exploits of the Golden Knight. I am the hero here!"

"You are a blowhard and a bully, Golden Knight," said his rival. "It shall yet be determined who is good and who is evil. On the field of honor."

Lunging with his sword, Sir Crispin shouted, "I shall best you, puppy. I always have and always shall."

Just as the Dark Knight pulled his weapon from under the sofa bed and prepared to defend himself, a massive pounding on the door stopped them both in their tracks.

"Uh-oh," Tuesday whispered.

If she'd thought it was awful waking up to find a sword fight at the foot of her bed, Kally knew it was nothing compared to what she faced now.

The wrath of Mrs. Krasselbine.

Chapter Four

Ka-blam.

The noise level went up a notch. Apparently Mrs. Krasselbine had decided to switch to her cane instead of injuring her fist on the door.

"Is this an enemy, my lady?" The Dark Knight fingered his sword. "Dare I hope 'tis the wizard who cast this enchantment, imprisoning you in this tower? He shall be begging for mercy at the end of my blade."

"Ha!" the Golden Knight chimed in. "I can slice any enemy into bits before your sword dares leave its scabbard, puppy."

"I can fillet any enemy and serve him for dinner before—"

"Stop it," Kally ordered. "This isn't a contest. Nobody is slicing or filleting anyone."

"Open this door," a quivery voice yelled. "Open this door and let me see what all the racket is!"

Kally closed her eyes and pretended she was somewhere else.

Ka-blam. Blam. Blam. If there was still one person on the fifth floor who hadn't been awakened by the knights' commotion, Mrs. Krasselbine was making sure they were up now.

And with those loud blows to her door, Kally saw life as she knew it going down the drain. Lease broken, eviction proceedings commenced, sanity in question, daughter taken away and given to irresponsible ex-husband...

But she was not going to think about any of that. Not just this minute. She had been in tough spots before and she had always found a way out. Of course, none of her scrapes had been quite *this* weird, but still...

"Open the door!" shouted the old woman.

"I'll be there in a sec," Kally called, stalling for time. "We're not, um, up. Or dressed."

Now what? Kally stiffened her spine. She would think of something.

She glanced at the two men, stalwart inside their shiny suits of armor, their swords at the ready, then at her daughter, looking trustingly to her for guidance, and finally at the door, where cranky old Mrs. Krasselbine was whaling away. *Think,* she commanded herself. But what could she do? There was no place to hide one large man, let alone two, in this tiny apartment. Under the bed, in the closet, the bathtub...

Even if she could strip them down to their skivvies, it would be a tight fit. But in full armor? Forget it. No, neither the closet nor the bathtub nor the bedroom would accommodate massive Sir Crispin's breastplate, let alone his whole body. And there was certainly no time to dump the armor.

No place to hide.

Except in plain sight. *Of course.*

"Okay," Kally said quickly, quietly, "Tuesday, help Sir Crispin put his helmet on, and then stick him over by the kitchen. And then, Sir Crispin, you have to keep your mouth shut. Not a peep, got it? Stand where Tuesday tells you, just like a statue." She hesitated, trying to figure out when statues were invented. "You do know what a statue is, don't you?"

He nodded, allowing himself to be led to the kitchen counter. Kally winced as each heavy metal foot fell, but she had other fish to fry.

"But what do I do with you?" she demanded of the Dark Knight, snatching up the pieces of his helmet as she spoke. Because she had removed the visor, his face would be right there for anyone to see. With sudden inspiration, she smiled. "We'll put it on backward. What are the chances Mrs. Krasselbine will know the back of one of these from the front?"

"Backward?" he sputtered. "You are suggesting that I, a knight of the realm, face a foe with my helmet on backward?"

Kally steered him over toward the wall. "Didn't anyone ever tell you that discretion is the better part of valor?"

"Daring and boldness, perhaps. But discretion? What has that to do with valor?" His dark eyes clouded, but Kally just handed him his metal glove.

She tried to ignore that penetrating gaze, pretending he was not staring a hole in her nightshirt. "Put it on. And breathe carefully. I don't want you passing out. It will make a big noise."

She could tell his fuse was getting shorter by the

minute. Some nasty little part of her was provoking him on purpose, but it was just too bad. Nobody had warned her that knights in shining armor were going to be such a royal pain. Although now that she thought about it, they were pretty testy in the stories, always getting into fights and quarrels, weren't they?

"All done," Tuesday said happily, sitting on the bed to hide the nasty slash in the mattress. "You are so smart, Mommy. We're going to pretend they're like those suits of armor at the museum, aren't we? Like a turtle shell without any turtle."

"Exactly." She backed toward the door, surveying the two "suits." As long as they didn't move or speak, everything should be fine. "Okay, Tues, I'm going to open up. Ready?"

Nodding, she flashed her mom an okay sign.

Kally took a deep breath and slid the chain, unbolted the lock and swung open the door. "What is it?" she asked, trying hard to act sleepy and innocent. She yawned loudly. "Oh, it's you, Mrs. Krasselbine. We were asleep. Is something wrong?"

"Well, you certainly took your time getting to the door, Mrs. Malone." Steam was practically coming out of the old woman's ears. "What was going on in there? Crashing and bashing and clanking. Why, anyone would think you were sinking the *Titanic* in there!"

Not even close, Kally thought. She opened the door a bit more, praying the knights would stand steady and not rattle as they breathed. "I have no idea what you mean," she lied baldly. "Tuesday and I were sound asleep until we heard the pounding on the door."

"Asleep? You expect me to believe that?" The old lady arched her thin eyebrows well into her forehead. "There was enough of a racket up here to wake the dead and send them packing."

"Would you like to see? There's nothing going on." Kally opened the door another sliver. "Just like earlier. Maybe you should have your hearing aid checked, Mrs. Krasselbine. I think it's making noises of its own."

"I don't wear a hearing aid. And I know what I heard."

"Then maybe it's the pipes in the building. Maybe your son should look into fixing them."

"That was no pipe." Peering inside, Mrs. Krasselbine wedged her cane against the door, presumably to keep Kally from shutting it. With a sniff, she hauled herself over the threshold, stepping in warily, focusing on a knocked-over end table and lamp Kally hadn't noticed in the rush. "Looks like quite a disturbance to me."

Quietly, Kally scooted over and righted the furniture. "I must've bumped into those on the way to the door."

But her nosy neighbor just glared at her, unwavering. "Turn on the light so I can see."

Kally gave the place a quick glance to see what else she'd missed, but it was too late now. Reluctantly, she switched on the small lamp near the door, the softest light available.

It wasn't enough.

"Ack!" squawked Mrs. Krasselbine. "What's that?"

Kally tried to distract her by saying, "Oh, you know Tuesday, don't you? Wave to Mrs. Krasselbine, hon."

Dutifully, the child waved a hand and smiled broadly. She leaned forward a little, swinging her legs, securely hiding the telltale gash from the sword fight.

"Not her," the old lady retorted. "I mean those things, those whaddya-call-'em, tin men, over by the wall. They weren't here earlier."

"Oh, *those*." Kally improvised a story on the fly. *Brad,* she thought suddenly. *Something to do with Brad. Mrs. Krasselbine always liked him.* "Those are a, uh, gift. From my ex-husband. Somebody, well, somebody gave them to him for a movie he did and he didn't have a place to put them, so he asked me to hold on to them for him."

It was a ridiculous story, but Kally stumbled on. "Yes, that's right. Just helping Brad out of a jam. You remember Brad, right?"

The woman squinted unpleasantly, tromping over to get a closer look. "Yes, I do remember your dear ex-husband," she murmured. "A real gentleman. Shouldn't have let him get away, if you ask me. Very promising young man. Why, he always had a kind word. Carried my groceries. And such a nice smile." And then she whacked the Dark Knight right on the shin with her cane.

Kally held her breath. But he didn't topple. He didn't even swear or lash out. He just stood there, like a champ, as if he really were an objet d'art and not an overheated, uncomfortable man with a backward tin can on his head. She silently promised to try to be nicer to the Dark Knight.

"That one's dented," the old woman said acidly. "Not worth much like that."

And then she used the tip of her cane to jiggle the bottom edge of the helm, balanced so precariously on his head. Kally's heart leaped into her throat. All the way across the room, she could hear Tuesday gasp as the silver helmet began to sway. If anybody even breathed, it was going to fall off.

Without even thinking, Kally slid between Mrs. Krasselbine and the Dark Knight. She set a hand casually on the fragile helm, holding it in place.

"You know how these things are. Not very steady." Behind her, hidden by her body, one gauntleted hand slid up and gave her a meaningful pinch on the bottom. She let out a small yelp, but covered quickly, edging out of range. Forget being nicer—she made a mental note to smack the Dark Knight when this was over. "I think this one may have been damaged in shipping. I'll have to tell Brad to look into that."

"Not going to leave them stacked against the wall, are you?" Mrs. Krasselbine inquired, finally backing off. "They look pretty stupid, if you ask me."

"I haven't decided yet." Kally yawned loudly, hoping to give her nasty neighbor a hint. Or at least get her away from the knights.

The old meddler was likely to poke a finger inside a breastplate next. What would she do if she encountered warm, firm male flesh? The shock might kill the old bat.

Kally cast a surreptitious look behind her. What did they wear under there, anyway? She couldn't see anything. The Dark Knight's suit was beautifully made, without gaps, without any hint of cloth between his hinges. Surely they had to wear something. Although she had heard that Scotsmen in kilts…

"Okay," she said abruptly, ready to get this show on the road and stop thinking about what the Dark Knight was or was not wearing under there. "Listen, Mrs. Krasselbine, if there's nothing else, we need to get back to bed. Because it's very late, you know."

"Those things may be too heavy for the floor here," the old woman insisted. "That might be a violation of the lease."

"I think I'm allowed to have decorations in my own apartment."

But Mrs. K shook her head, mussing her tight little hairdo. "I don't know. They're awfully heavy."

It was a standoff.

Finally, Mrs. Krasselbine announced, "I'll just have a look around. See if you're hiding anything else." And she disappeared into the tiny bedroom.

Thank goodness. Without thinking, Kally sagged against the Dark Knight. Bless his silver hide, he held her weight without a whimper. It was reassuring to feel the cold silver of his chest against her back and the steady pressure of his hard arms as they came around her.

"Let the old biddy snoop as much as she wants to," Kally whispered, patting his forearm. "As long as she leaves you guys alone."

And then she realized she was being held in a rather nice embrace by a suit of armor. She straightened, forcefully pushing his arms to his sides. She made a pretense of going to check on Mrs. Krasselbine as the old woman stomped all over, jabbed her cane into every nook and cranny and found nothing. Finally she sailed right past the armor and toward the door.

As Kally followed, antsy to close the door on the old woman once and for all, Mrs. Krasselbine turned for one final shot. "This isn't over," she announced, waggling her cane in the air. "I know you've got something going on in here, and I mean to find out what it is. Suits of armor in the middle of the night. Hrmph."

Kally shut the door smartly, sinking against it only when she was sure the coast was clear. "Dodged a bullet," she murmured. But for how long?

For all she knew, there *was* a prohibition in her lease against suits of armor. There was definitely a clause in there about not having extra people staying for any length of time without the landlord's permission. So what was she supposed to do? Just casually mention that she had two storybook knights holed up in her apartment for however long it took to figure out what to do with them?

Kally shoved her bangs off her face with one hand. "What a mess."

"Mommy, come on," Tuesday interrupted, scampering over to grab her hand. "Sir Crispin took his helmet off and he's liable to start clomping around again."

When her mother didn't answer, the little girl leaned in closer, whispering rapidly. "Where are they going to sleep, Mom? Because my bed is too little for either one of them, and I don't think they'll want to go together on your bed because, remember, they're mortal enemies.''

''I hadn't really thought that far ahead.'' She felt like saying, *You know, it is three o'clock in the morning, and I could use a nap here before I have to make any big decisions.* It was outrageous to consider letting two grown men, perfect strangers, stay overnight. No man had slept here since the divorce. Was this the time to start taking in uninvited guests?

''Come on, Mommy,'' Tuesday coaxed.

''But, sweetie, they can't stay here. We don't have anywhere to put them. And we don't know them. They could be criminals or something.''

''They're knights,'' Tuesday protested. ''Sworn to uphold the honor of women and protect the weak and helpless as they go around righting wrongs and being brave and slaying dragons. They won't hurt *us.*''

''Oh, Tues...''

''No, Mom, it's true.'' Her daughter's eyes were wide and plaintive. ''And besides, if you make them leave, it would be awful. They don't know anything about how it is here. They know about princesses and towers and stuff, not real things, not like subways and criminals and cabs. Mommy, *please.*''

Tuesday had a point. They could hardly kick fictional characters out onto the street in the middle of the night. What could she say? Go clomp into the lobby of the Plaza and see if they take the Arthurian Express card? Go camp out in the park, but be careful not to get mugged for the precious metals in your outfits?

''You're right,'' she said finally. ''So let's get them

out of the armor and figure out where to put them till morning. Maybe a good night's sleep will clear things up."

Or maybe they wouldn't be here when she woke up. Now that was an incentive to get to bed, wasn't it?

Kally rose, took Tuesday's hand and crossed to her suits of armor. Both men had removed their headgear and were impatiently waiting for her, casting ill-tempered glances at each other.

Sir Crispin had every hair in place, while the Dark Knight looked a little overheated. But that was no surprise, given the way he'd been wearing his helmet. His disagreeable mood lent him a certain fire, especially the way a few damp, dark tendrils clung to his cheek, the way his jaw clenched and his black brows drew together. Even given the golden competition, the Dark Knight was one attractive man.

"Let's get you out of there," she said.

Oops. Kally stopped in her tracks. For all she knew, he'd be naked when she peeled him out of his metal shell. There was no way she was even going to ask the question with her child in the room. So she said, "But first, Tuesday is going to bed. You guys can relax for a sec—quietly, please. When I get back, the three of us will discuss what we need to do in terms of your, um, attire." *Or lack thereof.*

"Aw, Mom, I want to help!"

"No, you're going to bed. It's very late. I will be coming in in a little while because it looks..." She gave the knights and their relative size a quick once-over. *No room at the inn...* "It looks like I'll be sleeping with you tonight."

"I don't want to go to bed," her daughter said, but Kally was already dragging her off.

"Just close your eyes and try to be creative about what we're going to do with them in the morning." Brooking no nonsense, she tucked the child into bed. "I have faith in you. You'll come up with something to get the knights out of Mommy's hair, won't you?"

"But Mommy, I like them in our hair."

Kally shook her head. Of course Tuesday wanted to keep them. She always *had* wanted a pet. But this was a bit more difficult than a hamster or a guppy.

She closed the door with a crisp click, not really ready to go back in and do battle, but as ready as she was going to get.

The Dark Knight was pretty much where she'd left him, cradling his gauntlets and his battered helmet in the crook of one arm. But Sir Crispin had arranged himself artfully against the edge of the sofa bed, and he was in the process of removing his breastplate, revealing a sort of cottony sweatshirt item with all kinds of dangly strings on the arms. Kally sighed with relief. So they *did* wear under-armor garments. Thank goodness.

She knew she shouldn't, but she spared a moment to admire the Golden Knight, all flowing locks and brawny muscles. She couldn't help it—the man really was stunning. His mighty chest strained against the soft, sky blue fabric of his shirt—just right to set off his eyes—as he bent to undo various gears and gizmos that confined him.

"Lord's mercy," he muttered, rubbing at the golden surface over one knee and one shoe. "My poleyn and my sabaton—ruined! Scraped and scarred, and with no squire to polish them. It is a catastrophe!'' He sent a murderous glance to the other knight, growling. ''This is your doing, you villain.''

But the villain in question glowered right back. ''Have you not comprehended that the Lady Kallista has asked us to keep our silence rather than face the return of the crone from below? Speak no more, churl.''

Kally smiled when she heard ''the crone from below.'' It fit Mrs. Krasselbine to a T. Meanwhile, her momentary appreciation of the Golden Knight's good looks evaporated in the face of his less than scintillating personality. Okay, so he looked like a god. But inside, all he cared about was how shiny his armor was and whether his hair was mussed.

Catastrophe, ha! She could give him chapter and verse on catastrophe, and a scuffed shoe wasn't it.

Once again, she was struck by how different things were than the book had led her to believe. Mr. Drop-Dead-Gorgeous, Flash-and-Dash Hero had a pea brain, while the supposedly vile knave kept surprising her with how much he had on the ball. Except for pinching her and calling her a wench, of course.

''Excuse me, my lady,'' that same vile knave interrupted. ''If it's not too much trouble, and if you are quite through fawning over the Golden Dunderhead over there, I would appreciate some assistance disarming.''

''I wasn't fawning. I was just...well, nothing.'' *Gee, that was a snappy put-down,* she chided herself.

"So what help do you need? Sir Crispin took his stuff apart by himself. Why can't you?"

Stiffly, he said, "Each warrior's armor is different, my lady. And I seem to have been badly enough dealt with in our small skirmish to be unable to manage it myself."

It took a moment to translate that into modern English. Badly dealt with...unable to manage...

"You're hurt?" Kally rushed to his side. "Where?"

"No, I am not injured," he murmured, his deep, disturbing gaze searching hers. "I fear it is only my pride and my plates that have suffered. Although I do find your concern most gratifying."

She didn't know what to say. When he was being sarcastic and snide, she could snap back. *That* she was used to. But how was she supposed to react when he sounded torchy and sweet, when his eyes captured and held her this way? It was positively...unsettling.

"Just tell me what to do," she said finally.

Wordlessly, he handed over the long metal gloves and the helmet, and she looked around for somewhere to stash them.

"Well, why not?" she muttered, taking a few steps and thrusting them on top of a pile of mittens and hats in the tiny front closet. While she was there, she pulled out a pillow and some blankets for whichever one of the knights decided to bunk on the floor. Behind her, she could hear Sir Crispin fall into the bed with a thump.

When she turned, she saw the big lug himself, still wearing his shoes and what looked like a tunic and tights as he sprawled across the bed. He was already snoring.

"I guess the issue of who gets the bed is decided." She sent the Dark Knight a mischievous glance. "Although we could roll him off onto the floor if you want to."

"That won't be necessary. I am quite accustomed to sleeping rough, and your floor looks softer than most." Lifting one silver arm, he added, in a meaningful tone, "Now if you would be so kind as to disarm me..."

"I'm coming, I'm coming." Gingerly, Kally edged in as close as she dared, dropping the bedding at his feet. "No pinching or poking of any kind, however."

"I beg pardon, m'lady. I was sorely provoked."

She frowned, fooling with one of his buckles, which seemed to have gotten bent out of commission. "I'm sorry she whacked you like that. But thank you for not whacking back."

"I pondered your notion about discretion and valor. Quite a sensible idea, I fancy."

When she happened to look up, she hesitated. Was that a smile playing around the narrow lips of the wickedest knight in Christendom?

Kally glanced away, busying herself with the strap around his waist. "Okay, so what seems to be the trouble? I undid all the things that hold the back and front together on your chest protector thing."

"You refer to my cuirass, my lady. By misfortune, the pauldron, that is, the, er, shoulder protector, is quite unyielding. It appears to be stuck as tight as the Sword in the Stone. And until I get the pauldron off,

I cannot remove the cuirass. And with the cuirass on, I cannot remove the cuisses.'' At her baffled expression, he explained, ''We have to get rid of this—'' he thumped his chest ''—before we can tackle these.'' And he tapped one long thigh.

''Oh.'' She swallowed, nodding. ''Chest before, um, thighs. Sure.'' Was he really proposing she go poking around his thighs?

''The pauldron is quite immovable. If you could...'' He craned his neck, trying to get a better look at the wide silver shoulder guard.

''Wait a sec. I'll get the can opener and the pliers again. Did I ever find WD-40?''

As she scrambled to get her Ms. Fix-It supplies together, he inquired, ''What is a sec?''

''A sec is a second. Sixty seconds to a minute. Sixty minutes to an hour. Don't you guys have clocks on that scale?''

''I am familiar with the concept,'' he said dryly.

After stripping off his gloves, he unhooked the various pieces on his arms while she worked on the jammed shoulder rivet. She couldn't help noticing the feel of his warm breath wafting past her ear, or the curiosity in his rapt gaze.

Even concentrating, she still couldn't get a clear view of the tiny gizmo on his shoulder, not even on tiptoe.

She considered. ''It might help if you could maybe sort of get down on your knees. Can you do that?''

''Kneel?'' A dark eyebrow arched. ''I think I can manage.''

Except that when he started to move, his large, metallic shoe came perilously close to her bare foot, and she squealed. He must have thought he'd stepped on her, because he reacted quickly, jumping back. But his foot fell on the pillow she'd dropped, and he started to slip.

All she could think of was the noise if that whole pile of tin hit the ground, and she grabbed him. She caught his arms, but he was too heavy to hold up, more than heavy enough to pull her over, too.

Luckily, they landed on the pillow and blanket with no more than a dull thud.

Unluckily, she ended up sitting right smack on top of him. Dead center. Straddling his hips.

Kally tipped her head just enough to give her a very good view of his bittersweet-chocolate eyes. Was that a spark of mischief she saw there?

He thought it was funny. And she felt like a demented cowgirl riding a stallion at the rodeo.

Chapter Five

"Please hold still." His midnight-dark hair spilled behind him as he attempted to rise, to catch her. "Please. Remain still."

"If you laugh, you're a dead man," she muttered.

"I am not laughing."

But there was a spark of something in his eyes. If not mischief, what?

Kally refused to think about it. She gulped, taking stock. His armor was very cold between her thighs. How had she ended up straddling him this way, with her knees next to his hips and her nightshirt dangerously scrunched up?

"Wait. Just a...sec." He winced. "I fear you are making this worse."

"Sorry," she whispered, trying to wiggle her nightshirt down to a reasonable level of protection. "But you know, this isn't my fault."

"It's moot to assign fault at the moment. But since we find ourselves in this position, perhaps we should use it to our advantage."

Kally was practically expiring from the precariousness of this, ahem, position, and she wondered again just how innocent this supposed stranger in a strange land was. "What do you mean, use it to our advantage?"

"Your pardon, m'lady, but now that we are situated thus, you can certainly reach my shoulder, can you not?"

If this was a scam to get her on top of him, he was awfully good at making it look accidental. "Well, that is true," she admitted, giving him the benefit of the doubt. "Here, let me look."

As delicately as possible, she levered herself up a bit, sort of sliding along his body. She did her best to ignore the proximity of his face to her chest as she bent to push the stubborn rivet along its little slot, but she couldn't miss the warm strength of his hands on her backside as he held her steady.

It wasn't easy, and she knew she was flushed and breathing funny, but she did the best she could.

She was so tired and so mentally hazy by this point, it didn't really seem to matter that she could feel the rise and fall of his chest under her thighs every time he took a breath.

Well, not much, anyway.

Finally, she got the damn thing to move—it was sort of like the catch on a jewelry box she'd once had that always got stuck—and she leaned back, satisfied. "There!"

He sat up partway, still holding her, and lifted off the shoulder piece that had caused so much trouble. "I am much obliged, Lady Kallista. That is much better."

Much better for whom? "Just Kally," she mumbled, not feeling much like a lady at the moment.

She knew she had to get off this man, and fast. She rolled to the side and off his lap, her fingers positively flying as she helped him undo various leather straps and rivets and hooks that held him together. This late at night, this far into a nightmare, it was amazing her coordination was working at all, but she pushed on. It was like unlocking a puzzle, but finally, blessedly, all they had was a pile of silver pieces and one large man, looking very dishy in a black tunic made of thick, soft cotton over still-silver legs.

"I, uh, think you can get the rest yourself," she murmured, staring at his thighs. The straps appeared to be buckled between his legs, and there was no way she was venturing in there, even if he begged. He could sleep in the blasted things.

But he sat on the pillow, apparently content to unhook his leg pieces himself. With a sigh of relief, he pulled off separate thigh, knee, calf and shoe plates and then leaned back, a free man.

It was funny how much bigger he looked without the armor. Or maybe it was just that he wasn't dwarfed by gigantic Sir Crispin. But sitting there, his eyes dark and unreadable, his mane of thick mahogany hair spilling over his tunic, he looked a lot more intimidating than she would have thought.

Intimidating. And sexy as hell.

There was something different about a man—even an imaginary one—in a dim, quiet apartment when you were all alone, just the two of you. It stirred dangerous embers, made her want to sink against him and feel the warmth of his arms.

He did look warm. And strong. And...

Her heart beating a little too rapidly, Kally tried to think cool, reasonable, *daytime* thoughts. Nothing about running her hands through that gorgeous hair. Not a thing about the breadth of his magnificent shoulders under the soft tunic. Not even one tiny thought spared for his moody eyes, his strong, elegant jaw, his narrow, sculpted lips, just now tweaking into a knowing smile.

Knowing? He knew she was watching him, devouring him with her eyes.

It had been too long since she'd been with a man, that was all. Much too long.

Weakly, she said, "Well, since you're, um, *obviously* doing, well, *fine,* I think I'll get to bed—I mean, *sleep.*"

But he just sat there, gazing at her while she gazed at him. Was that her willpower she felt melting away like ice cream in July?

All she could hear was the thump of her erratic pulse and the soft, steady rasp of his breathing.

This is insane.

Words began to spill out of her before she could stop them. She always did have a tendency to babble when she was nervous.

"Okay, so you've got a pillow and a blanket and you said the floor was okay and I'm taking you at your word because there's really no other choice, well, I suppose other than the bathtub. If you really want the bathtub, it's all yours, but it will be kind of hard and cold, so I suggest the floor right here because at least it's carpeted—"

"Kally," he interrupted. He rose to his knees and caught her hand between his.

Not *lady,* just *Kally.* It sounded...delicious. She whispered, "Y-yes?"

His eyes never left her. His skin felt hot and tingly next to hers. So very real.

"Kally, I want to..."

She closed her eyes, feeling rather than seeing him stand up, hovering beside her. It was bizarre, but she knew what he meant to say. *I want to...kiss you.*

And she wanted it, too.

"I want to..." But instead he finished, "Thank you." And he bent and kissed her hand, his lips sweet and soft against her skin.

Chivalry. Kally's knees turned to water. She couldn't breathe. She couldn't handle this.

Grabbing her hand away, she whirled and beat a hasty retreat to the bedroom. Safe inside, she locked the door, then scooted into the small, narrow bed with her daughter.

Tuesday was sleeping with a book clasped against her innocent cheek. A large, robin's-egg blue book, accented with gilded letters. Kally didn't have to look at the title. She knew. *Sir Crispin, the Golden Knight of Yore.*

With a shiver, she inched it out, careful not to wake the child, careful not to open the book, not even accidentally. If she read so much as a word, who knew what would come out next? A fire-breathing dragon?

A three-headed ogre bigger than her whole apartment building?

So she hid it under the bed, under a couple of shoe boxes and a cardboard container of Tuesday's winter sweaters.

Tomorrow she would deal with it. Tomorrow she would deal with all of this.

She hoped.

"MOMMY," Tuesday called brightly. "Time to wake up. I made breakfast."

It sounded so normal she thought for a minute that it had all been a bad dream. Surely when she stumbled out of bed, she would find nothing but her daughter and the Sunday *Times*.

But then she heard someone thunder, "You poach upon my victuals at your peril, you villainous churl!"

Villainous churls didn't exactly exist in her world. Which meant the knights and their armor were still here.

Kally groaned and pulled the pillow over her head.

"Mommy!" Tuesday said again. She danced all the way into the room. "Time to get up."

"What are you wearing?" Kally sputtered. "Last year's Halloween costume?"

Tuesday shrugged. The cardboard cone on her head, left over from her Halloween princess costume, waggled as she moved, stretching the elastic band under her chin. She'd found the rest of it, too—a leotard with a long net skirt over it, but as princessy as she got.

"Tuesday, put on your regular clothes this instant."

"Uh-uh. I like it." She tiptoed out the door, sticking

her head in long enough to say, "Come *on!* I want you to see what I made. Something special."

"What you made? You mean breakfast?" With images of blackened waffle irons and raging fires filling her mind, Kally jumped out of bed and ran for the kitchen. Sometimes there were scarier things than crazy knights. And Tuesday cooking breakfast was one of them.

"Look, Mommy," her daughter announced proudly. "The Round Table!"

Kally paused in mid-step. Round Table, huh? Well, the minuscule table that just barely fit into the nook they called a kitchen *was* round. It looked even tinier with two large men hulking over it, eating brightly colored cereal out of kiddie-size bowls.

"You gave them Fruity Pebbles?" she inquired, astonished. "And they're eating it? And why is your globe in the middle of the table?"

"Well, I brought out the globe so I could show them where we are," Tuesday explained. She rolled her eyes. "But Sir Crispin doesn't believe me."

As he shoveled in cereal, he managed to pause long enough to say, "Bah! As if anyone would believe this tale of men living on a round ball. Why, we would tumble right off! Everyone knows the world is but a platter, with dragons and sea monsters around the edges." He jammed his spoon in the bowl, sloshing milk in his eagerness for more Fruity Pebbles.

"You're getting milk on your place mat." Tuesday scurried over to pull a wedge-shaped piece of construction paper from under his plate. "It's what I wanted to show you, Mommy. See? Like the other Round Table."

"Oh, that's lovely, darling." Kally examined the triangular paper that read, in very loopy, bright yellow letters, Sir Crispin, the Golden Knight.

"More," the Golden Knight declared, holding out his empty bowl.

Tuesday scowled at him. "There isn't any more. You ate it all." Under her breath, she added, "And you spilled on my place mat and you didn't even say you were sorry."

"He ate it all? But that was a new box."

"I know." Her daughter stuck her small hands on her hips. "The Golden Knight is piggy, Mommy."

The Dark Knight was a bit more circumspect. He gave her a wan smile as he pushed away from the table. "Interesting," was all he said. Sir Crispin didn't stand on ceremony, just reached over and snatched the Dark Knight's uneaten cereal, quickly devouring that, too.

"I guess I better make a new place mat for Sir Crispin, since this one got spots on it."

Tuesday trudged off to get her markers and start over, and she looked so downcast that Kally told her, "Maybe we can have your place mats laminated at the copy shop, so they'll last longer." And then she realized what she'd said.

Last longer? As in, how long? As in, *How long would they be staying?*

"Have you not a crock of porridge or a joint of meat, not even a hunk of brown bread?" the Golden Knight demanded. "A knight of the realm cannot break his fast with such paltry provisions as these." He balanced a stray Fruity Pebble on the end of his mighty finger. "Mere trifles."

He was going to eat her out of house and home. And this was only his first meal!

"Mommy, look—my new place mat is going to be even better than the other one." Tuesday's face shone with enthusiasm. "I'm putting Sir Crispin's shield on this one. See the blue background and the gold lion?"

Kally found a smile for her daughter. "Just great, hon."

"Have you no sustenance for a ravening man?" Sir Crispin complained.

Tuesday whispered, "We don't have any more cereal, but you can find something to feed them, can't you, Mom? They're hungry. And we can't let them starve." Those round hazel eyes were so trusting, so guileless. Kally never could hold out against Tuesday when she put on her sweet and sincere face.

"I'll make them some toast," Kally said grudgingly. "And maybe I can dig up an egg or two."

"Thanks, Mommy. I love you."

"Don't overdo it, Tues."

A dozen eggs and two loaves of bread later, she was sorry she hadn't sent them out into the cruel world on their own. Crispin was the worst, of course, but the Dark Knight ate a decent amount, too. She couldn't blame them—they were huge, healthy men. But their appetites, as well as Tuesday's rampant enthusiasm, were wearing Kally out.

As they chowed down, she took her chance to sneak

away and get dressed. But never for a moment did the burden of her dilemma leave her.

What was she going to do with them?

Before she had time to think about it, she heard the opening salvo in a new round of their old battle.

"By the standing stones!" a loud voice she recognized as Sir Crispin's thundered. "This enchantment is well beyond your ken, Dark Knight. When two ladies as fine as these are imprisoned in a tower, left helpless and unprotected, with nary a liege lord nor a knight nor even a stripling boy to defend them, it lies to the likes of me—brave, stalwart and true—to end the spell and release them from their bonds."

"You are an oaf and an imbecile," answered the other. "It requires brain more than brawn to solve this riddle."

Did those two ever give it a rest? As if she needed saving. Well, actually, now that she thought about it, if anyone wanted to save her from *them,* she wouldn't complain.

Kally quickly finished drying her hair and went to referee the match. "Be quiet," she ordered from the bedroom door. "I don't want to have to tell you again."

But they gaped at her, mouths open.

The Dark Knight found his voice first. "You are quite fetching, my lady. But is it really necessary to disguise yourself in ragged boys' garments?"

"Disguise?" She glanced at her jeans and T-shirt. "These aren't boys' clothes. Everybody dresses like this here."

"But why?" asked Sir Crispin.

"I don't know! Because they do, that's why."

All she knew was that the two knights were driving her nuts. If she didn't come up with some scheme to get rid of them soon, she was afraid she might pack up her daughter and run away. Kally Malone had never run away from anything in her life, but these guys were pushing the envelope.

She lifted a hand to her pounding head. "Could you please just keep from arguing for five minutes? Finish eating and then you can use the bathroom."

"I already showed them how to flush," Tuesday announced proudly.

"Wonderful, darling." Her headache was getting worse. She couldn't help getting just a tad sarcastic. "Since we don't have any mountain streams handy, you'll have to figure out the shower on your own."

"I've accomplished that particular feat. It wasn't difficult," the Dark Knight muttered.

Was that amusement she heard in his voice? Curious, Kally glanced up, trying not to really, actually look at him. So far, she'd been avoiding his eyes.

Oh, dear. Yes, he was every bit as intense and arrogant and infuriating as last night, even with his thick hair damp from his shower and pulled into a ponytail with a bright green scrunchie no doubt supplied by Tuesday.

Scrunchie or no, one look was all it took. Last night came flooding back in all its bizarre, embarrassing detail. Her knees felt weak, her pulse jumped, her face flushed.

What was she going to do?

She was starting to get desperate. *I have to get rid of them. But how?*

"Maybe there's an answer in the book," she muttered, grasping at straws. Maybe there was some page she didn't get to where they spelled out how to lose a couple of pesky imaginary knights.

The Dark Knight narrowed his eyes. "What did you say?"

"Nothing." She turned to her daughter. "Tues, you keep making place mats. I'll be back in a little while."

"Are there more foodstuffs?" Sir Crispin inquired from somewhere near his plate. He beamed at her, flashing so many pearly whites it was blinding. "A flagon of ale would also be appreciated."

Kally backed away before *she* picked up a sword. "I haven't got time for this. Tuesday, show him what's in the fridge. I have to..."

Figure out how to get rid of them. Sir Crispin the Oaf, and the Dark Knight with his mysterious glances. Well, together they were too much for anyone to handle.

As Sir Crispin began to scrounge in the refrigerator, Kally ran for the bedroom, shut the door and hit the floor, hunting under the bed for the mysterious volume she had hidden there. She felt a tingle of fear as her fingers touched the cool leather cover, and she had to force herself to open the thing up.

"Be brave," she ordered herself. "It has to be done."

Open. One page. And then two. With a sigh of relief, Kally realized no monster was going to pop out. At least not yet.

As she sat on Tuesday's bed, poring over every line of *Sir Crispin, the Golden Knight of Yore,* she was again caught by the beauty of the illustrations and the lure of the prose. It was spooky to see someone she had met within its pages. But somehow the book version of Sir Crispin didn't seem as impressive now that she'd met him in the flesh.

Without realizing it, she found herself searching for more references to the Dark Knight, locating his black-etched armor and familiar form in the background of the pictures. There he was, peeking around trees, on horseback in the distance, always lurking somewhere.

She smiled, tracing his image with one finger. "Why, they did show his face," she whispered. Right there on page forty-three, almost off the edge of the illustration, you could definitely see those lean, saturnine features. She tipped her head to one side, staring at it. "That's funny. I could swear that picture wasn't in here before."

But she didn't allow herself to ponder it. A fresh burst of noise from the kitchen reminded her that she had a mission—to decipher the book's secrets, to find some clue to help her send them back, before they ate her into poverty, before they destroyed anything, before they got her sent to the loony bin.

Desperate, she read and reread the book, but there was nothing there. "Not even a clue," she said mournfully.

What next?

As she was sticking the book under the bed, Tuesday came barging in. "Mom," she declared, in a very tattle-tale voice, "Sir Crispin squeezed catsup on the

Dark Knight because he thought it was funny, and the Dark Knight is really mad, but he said he couldn't run him through because you told 'em not to make any noise. But I thought you should know."

"How am I supposed to think of solutions when those goons keep interrupting me? If you had to send me two knights," she said aloud to the powers that be, "couldn't it have been two who got along?"

Still, after getting all the way through the book twice, she had to admit the Dark Knight had his reasons for holding a grudge against Sir Crispin. Every time the poor guy turned around, the Golden Knight was humiliating him, tricking him, cheating him, thwarting him and thumping him. And now he'd squeezed catsup on him. Some hero.

"I think maybe we should make them play outside," Tuesday advised, taking her mom by the hand and leading her into the fray.

Right. Send a full-grown knight outside to play on the streets of New York. There were lots of weirdos out there, but none who said *Ods bodkins* and ran people through with swords. No, outside was probably not a good idea. She glanced ruefully at the Dark Knight. What was she going to do with him?

"Do you have a garment I might beg the loan of?" he asked, distastefully holding his soggy tunic away from his chest.

"No, not really." Ever since Brad moved out, her supply of man-size clothing was nonexistent. "Maybe a T-shirt."

After a moment, she rounded up one of her own shirts and sent him into the bathroom, unwilling to watch him change and even less willing to allow it in front of her daughter. She wasn't too surprised, though, when he returned with the T-shirt stretched taut across his broad shoulders, with a thin line of tanned skin showing between the bottom edge of the too-small shirt and the top of his pants. His trousers looked like drawstring sweatpants, except they fit more snugly than that. More like tights. And without the long tunic, there wasn't much of his body left to the imagination.

He was in very good shape, she'd give him that.

"I can't take much more of this," she murmured, her eyes glued to his narrow hips and long, sinewy thighs, to the stretchy fabric that hugged him, up and down.

"Mommy, that's too little," Tuesday scoffed.

Tuesday? *Yikes!* "Tuesday, please go in your room and read the book. Look for clues. Now. And lock the door. Oh, and change out of that princess outfit while you're in there." More to herself than to her daughter, she added, "I'm going to get the Dark Knight some baggier clothes."

The Dark Knight lifted one eyebrow but didn't say a word. He didn't have to. He knew darn well what he looked like in that outfit, and he was enjoying discomfiting her.

"Here," she said, retreating long enough to drag a faded flannel shirt out of the back of the closet. The elbows were completely worn through and half the buttons were missing, but it was better than nothing. "You can put this on for the time being."

As he shoved his arms into the sleeves, looking very

bemused by the shape of the garment, Kally stumbled to the phone. Whom could she borrow from? Brad, damn it. He was the only man she knew well enough to ask for his clothes, even if he was her ex-husband.

Thank goodness he answered on the first ring. Must've been expecting a call back. "Hey, it's me," she said without preamble, cradling the phone and facing away from the Dark Knight.

Brad was instantly wary, pouring on the charm. "Oh, Kal. What a nice surprise. So good to hear your voice. Look, I'm sorry I couldn't take Tuesday for the weekend. I had a chance to do a really significant part in the new Tom Cruise—"

"Yeah, I'm sure you did. I didn't call about that. The thing is, I need a favor." How to put this? Tentatively, she began, "You see, I have two visitors in from out of town."

That was an understatement.

"Two men," she added. "And one of them spilled something on his shirt, and I don't have anything to give him to wear until it dries. So I thought maybe you would come over and bring..." Might as well plan ahead. "Bring a couple of changes of clothing—three or four shirts and maybe some pants. Anything big, you know, baggy?"

"What?" Brad wasn't a good enough actor to keep the surprise and irritation out of his voice. "Let me get this straight—you have two male friends who don't have any clothes staying with you? What are they, strippers?"

"No, of course not." But she couldn't think of any way to explain this. And now she'd involved *Brad,* of all people, insatiably curious Brad, who couldn't stand it when interesting things happened to other people because it took attention away from him. He was going to want to know all the details and then he was going to have a fit. What was she thinking, calling Brad? "Forget it," she said quickly. "No big deal."

And she hung up, hoping that was good enough to keep him out of this mess. All she needed was for Brad to start snooping around, getting cranky, making dire predictions about her future.

"Were you speaking to someone through that apparatus?" the Dark Knight inquired. His brows drew together. "The sorcerers here are really quite extraordinary. With whom were you conversing?"

"I don't have time to explain the telephone or my ex-husband right now. I have to..." *I have to get rid of you!*

"Ex-husband?" The Dark Knight lifted a midnight brow. "You are a widow, m'lady? And this apparatus enables you to converse with the spirit world?"

"He's not dead, just...ex. Don't they have divorces where you come from? Separation, estrangement, Splitsville?" Didn't Arthur and Guinevere get a divorce? She thought she remembered something like that from Tuesday's books. "No, wait. The women just get sent off to be nuns or something, don't they?"

She didn't get a chance to find out.

"Mommy?" Kally whirled in time to see Tuesday poke her head out of the bedroom. "Can I come out yet?"

"No, go back. I told you to read the book and find clues."

"But I did."

"You did?" Kally didn't waste any time. She marched over there quick, edging herself into the bedroom and bringing Tuesday with her. With the door shut, she whispered, "Quick, honey, tell me. How do we put the knights back in the book?"

"Well, I don't know that."

Kally sat on the bed with a sigh. "Oh, I thought you meant there was some riddle or something in there that would make this all go away. I guess it couldn't be that easy."

"Sorry." Tuesday twirled on one toe. "All I meant was that it's the book, you know, that started it, so maybe, like, the book can fix it. Or where the book came from. Because if it's a magic book, with instructions or something, then maybe it would be good to know that."

"Know what?" Kally was thoroughly confused. "What do you mean?"

"Well, we got the book at the bookstore and Mr. Kew said funny things about how it was for both of us and we needed it or something. So I thought maybe he—"

Kally leaped to her feet. "Mr. Kew."

"Well, that's what I was—"

She grabbed her daughter and hugged her. "Mr. Kew sold us that horrible book, so he owes us an explanation—and a way out."

"Maybe." Tuesday shrugged her slender shoulders. "Maybe not."

"Let's keep our fingers crossed."

Kew's Curiosity Shop. Where Curiosity is our middle name.

It had to be the answer.

Chapter Six

Kally stood up, resolute. "Come on, Tuesday. We have a mission."

"A mission? Like a quest? Cool!" But Tuesday turned the wrong way and began to rustle around in her chest of drawers. "If we're starting a quest, I need to change my clothes."

"All right. But hurry up, okay?" Kally pushed open the bedroom door, already trying to figure out how to safely leave the knights while she and Tuesday went out in search of magic disappearing potions. Or whatever Mr. Kew had to offer.

She stopped in her tracks. Was that giggling she heard coming from the living room? Neither of the knights would've been able to manufacture a girlish tee-hee like that.

As Kally turned the corner, the Dark Knight strode over to meet her. But he didn't block the cozy scene on the sofa. Rosie, her bouncy blond next-door neighbor, was ensconced next to Sir Crispin, batting her eyelashes and giggling to beat the band. As usual, Rosie was wearing a neon-bright leotard that fit like glue. With her ample bosom and feminine curves,

Kally doubted whether anybody had accused Rosie of being disguised as a boy.

Trying not to panic, Kally cleared her throat to announce her presence. "Well, hello there. I didn't know anyone was here—I didn't hear the door." She managed a smile. "Just dropped by?"

"Hi, Kally!" Rosie bubbled. "The door was open, and I saw him—" she punched Sir Crispin lightly on the bicep "—so I decided to pop in for a minute."

How many minutes? What did he tell you? Kally wanted to shout.

"We've barely had time to say hello," Rosie said cheerfully. She jumped up from the sofa and bounced closer to Kally. "So who are these guys? Where'd you get them from? Are you going to introduce me?"

There was a long pause as Kally considered what she ought to say. Introductions? Oh, heavens.

Tuesday chose that moment to come racing out of the bedroom dressed in a pair of daisy-print leggings and a long yellow T-shirt. Except for the girlish fabric and a few ruffles around the hem of her shirt, her outfit was a decent facsimile of what the knights wore. No longer content to be a passive princess, she'd found a new role model, apparently.

And her entrance gave Kally just enough time to come up with something. Luckily, Rosie was none too bright, so whatever story she thought up didn't have to be spectacular.

She improvised. "Well, you've already met my friend Sir Crispin…er, Cris. Cris…" What to call him? *Sir Crispin, the Golden Knight.* Cris Golden?

No. "Cris Knight. He's a friend visiting from, um, Wales."

"A sir, huh? Like royalty or something. This one, too?" Rosie cooed, batting her eyelashes at the Dark Knight.

Kally swallowed. She'd just realized she had no idea what his name was, or even if he had one. "He's, uh..."

"Septimus," Tuesday whispered, pulling on her hand.

"Septimus?" Kally was astonished. How did Tuesday know? But the man nodded, confirming it.

"I've never heard of a Septimus before," Rosie said, tapping her generous mouth with one fingernail. She elbowed Kally. "So introduce me already. Septimus what? Is he from Wales, too?"

"Um, yeah, from Wales." Still hazy over the details, Kally tried to think up a last name for him. She couldn't call him Knight, too. As luck would have it, his shield, with its seven black birds against a field of red, was propped against the wall not far from where she stood. Looking at the shield, she blurted out, "Sparrow. Yes, that's right. Septimus Sparrow."

"Sparrow?" His eyes narrowed, and his voice went up a notch. "Sparrow?"

"Well, I—"

"Will you excuse us for a moment?" he asked the others. "I need to speak to Kally privately."

"I don't think so—"

But she had no choice. His hands firmly on her shoulders, he steered her between Rosie and Tuesday, straight into the tiny kitchen, where there was just enough room for the two of them to stand face-to-face, toe-to-toe between the sink and the stove.

In the main room, Kally heard Rosie say loudly, "So, Cris, how do you know Kally? How long are you staying?"

Oh, jeez. What was he going to say? "I have to go—" Kally tried to squeeze around the Dark Knight's hard, angry body.

But he interrupted, glaring daggers at her, moving to completely block her path. "Sparrow?" he demanded in a low, fierce tone. "The brave and mighty hawk adorns my shield, my lady. Do you really think so little of me that you would paint me as a *sparrow?*"

"Well, I..." But Kally didn't know what to say. Even though he was a fictional character, she was getting the idea that the Dark Knight—Septimus—had feelings. And now, here he was, madder than a wet cat, only inches away, his knees knocking hers if he so much as breathed, staring at her with deep, dark eyes.

He seemed awfully real all of a sudden.

Kally swallowed. The Dark Knight was a beautiful man in a sort of lean and hungry way. But what was she doing thinking about him that way?

And what was he doing, looking at her that way?

She didn't need a book to read the expression in his eyes. Irritation, yes. Exasperation. Maybe even a little wounded pride. And... And a very potent helping of desire.

His eyes devoured her, sweeping up and down, drinking her in. She felt the heat of his gaze as real as any lick of flame. And she didn't know what to think, what to do, where to move.

"I'm sorry," she whispered. "About the sparrow. I don't know my birds very well."

He didn't say it was okay or that he didn't mind. He didn't say anything.

Instead, he edged forward, pressing her back into the sink. Kally retreated, her eyes wide, as far as she could go. He paid no attention. Without a word, without a sound, he bent, hauled her into his arms and covered her mouth with his.

His lips were hard, hungry, demanding, and she more than responded. *Wow.* Was that greedy little moan coming from her?

Abruptly, he broke the kiss, dropping her onto the counter, and Kally gasped for air.

He arched one eyebrow and looked so smug she could've hit him.

"So," he murmured, "does that feel like the kiss of a sparrow?"

Kally blinked. But sparrows didn't even have lips. And Septimus definitely had lips. Wonderful, warm, persuasive lips.

Oh, God. This couldn't be happening.

Why couldn't she seem to catch her breath? And why did her body feel like it had just been melted over an open flame?

"I—I don't know what kind of animal you kiss like," she said breathlessly, allowing herself the teeniest, tiniest hope that maybe he would kiss her again and she could test more carefully this time. "But I'm willing to—"

Septimus apparently didn't care for her answer. Either that or he'd made his point. Because he turned on his heel and stalked out of the kitchen, leaving her standing there, trembling.

"Wait," Kally called after him. She couldn't believe this! She felt like stamping her foot. "How dare you ki— How dare you? And then just leave? I don't think so, buster."

As she cleared the partition into the living room, the rest of them—her daughter, Crispin, and Rosie—watched her with open curiosity.

Kally felt her cheeks flame. Could they tell she'd just been kissed in the kitchen?

"You shouldn't argue with your guests," Rosie said sweetly, making a tsk-tsk noise. She crinkled her nose. "Especially ones as cute as these."

"We weren't arguing." But she knew her injured tone and the storm clouds gathered on Septimus's face told a different story. Was he really still angry about the stupid name thing? She mumbled, "I said I was sorry."

"See, she said she was sorry," Rosie interjected, looping an arm through the Dark Knight's and pinching his cheek. "Time to kiss and make up."

As if she would ever kiss that insufferable man again. Not in a million years. But at the very mention of a kiss, her face flushed even hotter. "Kisses aren't necessary," she said stiffly.

Her bouncy blond neighbor didn't hear. She was already onto a new topic. "Just in case you guys need something, I want you to know I'm right next door." She squeezed Septimus, leaving his side long enough to wave at Cris. "So just give me a yell. Remember—Rosie, next door."

"Rosie?" Crispin swept his glorious mane behind him, leaping to his feet. "Were you christened so? Rosie? Have I apprehended correctly?"

"Oh, sheesh. I'm sorry. Didn't I tell you my name before? Rosie Donaldson, next door."

With a shout that took them all by surprise, Sir Crispin bounded across the room and threw himself into a kneeling position in front of her. His eyes shone with devotion as he took her hand in his.

"Sir Crispin, no," Kally said, but there was no stopping him.

He bent low over Rosie's hand, pressing it with fervent kisses. "My beloved," he cried. "The Fair Rosaminda."

Kally kicked herself for not seeing this coming. But how could she? Who would ever guess Crispin was dopey enough to mistake Rosie and her washboard abs for the sylphlike Rosaminda?

"Rosaminda?" the Dark Knight echoed softly. "Can it really be you?"

Not him, too. *Good grief.* And there was an unsteady thread in his voice Kally hadn't heard before. A thread she didn't like one bit.

"She's not the Fair Rosaminda," Kally tried to tell them. "She's just an aerobics instructor from next door."

"Oh, it's okay." Rosie looked slightly dazed. "If they both think I'm this Rosa chick, it's okay with me. Maybe I am." She shrugged her shoulders. "Who am I to say they're wrong?"

"Trust me. They're wrong," Kally said flatly.

With Crispin practically prostrate with adoration and Septimus looking as if he'd been hit over the head with a two-by-four, Kally was left to fume silently.

"Beautiful, divine Rosaminda," the Dark Knight whispered. "Now, finally, I understand why I was sent on this journey. To find you." And he took a step toward her, blocked only by the large golden body stuck to her hand.

What? The Dark Knight kissed *her* in the kitchen and then switched allegiance so fast? *Sent on this journey to find you...* Her hands curled into fists. She was definitely going to throttle him. She just hadn't decided how.

Meanwhile, Rosie gave Septimus a smile for his pretty words, and Crispin noted the exchange. He growled at his rival, "Fair Rosaminda is mine. I would never allow a cur like you to touch so much as one hair upon her flaxen head."

"It is not yours to decide, and never has been." Septimus bit the words out. "Unhand my lady, Golden Goat. Unhand her now."

His brows drew together and he looked quite fierce, as if he were more than ready to defend his position.

"Isn't it romantic?" Tuesday whispered, tugging on her mom's belt loop.

But Kally was burning. It wasn't that she was jealous or anything. So what if they'd both fallen for Rosie like a ton of bricks? Did she care? Ha!

No, it was the injustice of the situation that bothered her. Two knights, sworn to chivalry, and they were about as loyal as Benedict Arnold. What had happened to all their enthusiasm to break *her* spell? It hadn't taken them very long to lose sight of one quest and set their sights on a new one. A curvier, blonder one.

She crossed her arms over her chest. Not that she wanted them arguing about who got to free her from her tower prison. It was absurd. But still, they'd popped up in *her* living room, not Rosie's.

With that thought uppermost in her mind, Kally sidestepped both knights, took Rosie by the hand and attempted to shepherd her toward the door. In a voice so perky it made her ears hurt, she declared, "Time to go. Wouldn't want to overstay our welcome, would we?"

"Lady Kallista, I beg you," cried Crispin, crawling after her on his knees. "Now that I have spied the one true love of my heart, I cannot be parted from her so soon."

"She's just next door. You can visit her later."

"Yeah, guys, I really gotta go," Rosie said cheerfully, allowing herself to be pulled along. "It's fun being the Divine Miss Rose or whatever, but I've got to teach advanced step aerobics at one, so I can't hang with you right now. See you later, okay?"

"Later," Kally called out, shoving the blonde out and shutting the door.

"Rosaminda," Crispin breathed, gazing skyward, his hand pressed to his heart.

"Rosaminda," the Dark Knight echoed, in a far grimmer tone.

"Rosaminda," Kally muttered. *"As if."*

Sir Crispin leaped to his feet, whispering and gesturing like crazy. He looked as if he were being chased by bees, but Kally caught the gist of his animated conversation with himself—he was amazed that the Fair Rosaminda should turn up in this very same tower, and he vowed to break the enchantment once and for all. He paced back and forth, alternately despairing that he didn't know how and getting all moony and happy that he had caught a glimpse of the fair Rosaminda.

"Men," Kally groused.

On the other side of the room, the Dark Knight was intent and serious. Glowering at her. Again.

"Everybody's so cranky," Tuesday complained, looking from one face to the other.

Finally, Kally could take no more of the tension. She stalked next to Septimus and lowered the boom. "Stop it, okay? Staring daggers at me isn't doing any good, because I don't even know why you're mad. Is it because I got rid of Rosie? She is *not* Rosaminda. I promise."

Septimus said nothing, just kept glaring. Finally, he muttered, "You called me a sparrow in front of the Fair Rosaminda."

Kally rolled her eyes. "Are you still harping on that? Big deal! Get over it. It wasn't meant as an insult and it gave you no right to..."

She paused. What in the world did you call what had happened between them in the kitchen? Besides a rather steamy kiss that went absolutely nowhere because he turned tail and left just when things were getting good?

"You had no right to *accost* me in my own

kitchen.'' She was rather proud of herself for coming up with a positively knightly word.

''I did not accost you,'' he returned darkly.

''What does that mean, Mommy? Accost?''

''Nothing,'' she said quickly.

''Oh, come on, it does so. I know it means *something!*''

''I'll explain it later, Tuesday. Right now, Sir Septimus and Mommy are having a grown-up conversation.''

''You always say that.'' Grumbling, the little girl flopped onto the sofa in front of the TV.

Next to Septimus, Kally stood firm, waiting for her apology. ''I still say you had no right to...to do what you did.''

Grudgingly, he replied, ''I beg pardon, my lady. I did not intend to kiss you. It will not happen again.''

''What?'' Tuesday jumped from the couch. ''You and Septimus were *kissing,* Mommy? Is that what accost means? Why didn't you tell me? Did you kiss him? Like a friend, or like a, you know, boyfriend?'' She gasped. ''Did he kiss you like on 'Melrose Place'? No way!''

So many questions, so few answers. It took her a second to figure out what to say. Finally, a simple, only slightly defensive no seemed like the best course.

Tuesday wasn't convinced. ''No to which one?''

''No to all of them.''

Septimus began, ''I beg to differ—''

''Don't you dare differ,'' Kally interrupted, turning on him. Didn't he have any sense at all, for goodness' sake?

"But, my lady, I cannot lie. When I was knighted, I vowed—"

"Who cares what you vowed? There's a thing called manners, not to mention discretion. Remember, the better part of valor?" If she sounded snide, she didn't care. "Or did you already forget?"

"Does that mean you did or didn't kiss him?" Tuesday asked in confusion.

"I definitely did *not* kiss him," Kally avowed.

"My lady, is it really the best course to persist in falsehoods in front of the child? How shall she learn the virtue of truth?"

"Mommy, are you lying?"

"No, sweetheart. Of course not." She crossed her arms again and frowned at the Dark Knight. "Let's get this straight, buster. I didn't kiss you—you kissed me."

His brows drew together. "Buster? Is this akin to *sparrow?*"

Crispin roused himself from his Rosaminda-induced stupor long enough to catch a few of Kally's words. With an oath, he, too, joined the conversation. "Am I to understand that you have insulted Lady Kallista?"

"Yes!" Kally encouraged him. At least she had one champion.

But then Crispin continued, "And yet you dare to lay claim to the hand of the Fair Rosaminda after such perfidy? You are faithless and vile, Dark Knight! You are not fit to touch the hem of the Fair Rosaminda's gown. Upon my oath, you shall never come near her."

"Rosaminda was promised to me in good faith," his rival said between clenched teeth.

Tuesday interjected, "He's right, you know. Her father, old King Alardyce, betrothed her. It's right in the book."

Kally had heard enough. He admitted he'd kissed her, and yet he was still angling for someone else's hand. All of this within the space of a few minutes. He had the attention span of a hummingbird. Cris was right—Septimus was faithless and vile.

"My lady," the Dark Knight began, sweeping her with those deep, mysterious eyes.

"My lady, pay him no heed," urged Crispin, pushing in front of his rival. "Rather, tell me how to find the Fair Rosaminda again."

"I am not going to listen to any more of this," she declared, her head held high. "Tuesday and I—" she caught her daughter's hand "are getting out of here. We're going to..."

Find Mr. Kew and make him send you back to Camelot or Cape Canaveral or the Planet Zardoz, whatever's fastest.

"Go for a walk," she finished with as much dignity as she could muster.

The Dark Knight made a move in her direction. "I shall accompany you."

"Oh, no, you won't," Kally said forcefully.

"Surely it is unwise for a woman and child to travel alone, unescorted?" He gave them a wary glance. "Even if you are disguised as boys, the protection of a knight seems prudent."

Now she really felt like kicking him. "We're not disguised as boys, and we can take care of ourselves, thank you. I'm neither a scullery maid nor some wispy lady who sits around waiting for a knight to come along and get her out of a jam. If there are jams, I get myself out!"

"And your imprisonment in this tower? What of that?"

Kally raised a hand to her head. "If I were imprisoned, would I be going out right now?"

"No, I suppose not," Septimus said slowly. Behind him, Sir Crispin looked totally perplexed.

"Let's go, Tues," Kally ordered.

"But what will they do while we're gone, Mommy?" Tuesday asked in a small voice. She looked very worried.

"I don't know what they'll do, sweetheart. Maybe they'll..." What did knights do for relaxation, anyway?

As if reading her thoughts, Septimus spoke. "Play the lyre, practice for the joust, listen to a bard, watch a juggler or a fire-eater, woo a maiden, write a verse or two?"

"See?" Kally patted Tuesday on the head. "There are lots of things they can do."

"But, Mommy, I think they'll fight again and then here will come Mrs. Krasselbine..."

"Okay, so they'll take a vow not to fight. They can do that, right? These guys take vows all the time." She smiled at both knights, but they looked less than thrilled. In her best camp counselor tone, she ordered, "Pick up your sword, Sir Crispin. Upon your honor, yada yada, you promise not to fight while we're gone. Go ahead."

It was clear he didn't want to, but reluctantly, he

echoed her words. "Upon my honor as a knight of the realm, I vow to forswear fighting while Lady Kallista is away," he grumbled.

"You next," she told Septimus.

He lifted one dark eyebrow, and she had the feeling he was going to mock the whole process. But he knelt swiftly, laying his sword flat in front of her, gazing deep into her eyes.

"Upon my honor as a knight of the realm," he declared, with only a hint of sarcasm, "I take this solemn vow. Even if sorely provoked, even if the cowardly Golden Dunderhead shall, with neither rhyme nor reason, attack my person, I shall refrain from defending myself or taking the field of battle until Lady Kallista the Good and Wise shall return to this keep and advise me my vow is fulfilled. My lady," he whispered, and she couldn't tear herself away from the power of his gaze, "you have my word, my bond, my vow."

Kally was speechless. This knight stuff wasn't all bad. *You have my word, my bond, my vow.* She kind of liked the sound of that, especially in Septimus's deep, husky voice. She shivered.

Snap out of it, she told herself. He might have pretty words and a magnetic gaze, but it was all a sham. He'd do the same to Rosie if she were available. "You can get up now."

"Mommy," Tuesday interrupted, "they'll still need something to do while we're gone. 'Cause if they're just gonna sit here and be mad at each other, they'll get into a fight sure as shootin'. No matter whether they vow or not."

Kally agreed. She had a sudden inspiration—the

electronic baby-sitter. She turned on the TV. "It's like your own little storybook in a box. Lots of fun."

Sir Crispin wandered in front of the set, his baby blue eyes wide. "By the great hounds of Hadrian! There are wee folk entrapped in this chest. Yet they do not appear to be fairies. How was this done?"

Physics wasn't her strong suit. So she lied. "It's magic."

The Dark Knight straggled behind, but he, too, looked intrigued. "'Tis part of the enchantment, then? This is fearsome powerful sorcery."

"Sure. Why not?" Kally stuck in a video and prepared to leave before she regretted her decision.

But Tuesday tugged at her hand. "Mom, no! You can't put in *Camelot!*"

"Why not? I thought it would make them feel at home."

"Because," Tuesday whispered, "they don't know about Arthur and Guinevere and how—" she lowered her voice even further "—how it didn't work out."

"You don't think that's happened yet, back home?"

Tuesday shook her head vigorously.

"Okay, I give. How about..." Kally perused the stack. "*The Wizard of Oz.* That should be right up their alley." To the knights, she said, "Watch carefully. Take notes. We'll be back later."

Not waiting for any more objections, she grabbed Tuesday's hand and made for the door. She had never felt such relief to be leaving her apartment.

Chapter Seven

Tuesday was one grumpy girl. "You said we were going on a quest, Mommy. Trying to get rid of the knights is *not* a quest. It's...murder."

"Tuesday, please don't be overly dramatic. I'm having enough trouble with this as it is."

"But..." The little girl stopped in the middle of the sidewalk, getting angry glances from a woman with too many packages who had to sidestep her. "Won't you miss them if we make them go back in the book?"

"Miss them? No," she said immediately.

Even she knew she was protesting a bit too much.

Crispin? No, she wouldn't miss him. But Septimus...

She couldn't help thinking of the heated glances in the middle of the night, of his hard, long body underneath her as she unbuckled him from stem to stern, of that gorgeous midnight-dark hair spilling over his shoulders, of his lips, warm and soft against the back of her hand, against her mouth...

She closed her eyes. This had to stop. Had to go away. She lived a controlled, orderly life, full of her daughter and her work and her schedules. Knights and noise and commotion and lying on top of a man in the living room at three in the morning were not part of it.

Would she miss them? "Miss all the messes they make?" she asked aloud. "Hiding them from Mrs. Krasselbine? Will I miss their amazing consumption of food?"

"How about Septimus kissing you?" Tuesday asked slyly. "Nobody ever kisses you, Mom. I mean, except like me, like good-night, and that's not the same, not like on 'Melrose Place' when they're all gooey and stuff."

"You're not supposed to be watching 'Melrose Place,'" she said, but Tuesday was riding roughshod over her objections.

"Now that he kissed you, I bet you'll miss him after that."

"Well, I don't—" But she broke off. For all she knew, he was kissing Rosie even as she spoke.

Even more determined, she pulled her daughter along until they reached the wrought-iron railing in front of the bookstore. They both peered into the window from the street. But today there was no beckoning cat, no warm glow from inside. In fact, for the first time Kally could remember, the display window was completely empty.

The only things there were the faded gilt letters that read *Kew's Curiosity and Book Shop* and a small placard, turned to the Closed side.

"Not open," Tuesday announced, pulling at her mother to move along.

"Wait." The tingles had started again, tickling her

toes, making her slightly light-headed. As Kally gazed at the empty window, her dizzy feelings of anticipation and apprehension grew stronger.

And a hand reached out and flipped the sign to Open.

She swallowed. It took a second to quell the jitters, to close her eyes and focus on the sound of taxi horns and pedestrians' chatter. This *was* the real world. Not the twilight zone.

"Come on, Tues," she said finally. "It looks like Mr. Kew is in."

She didn't know why she took the stairs so slowly. Maybe because she still felt edgy and weird. Or maybe because Tuesday had reminded her of Septimus's kisses, and a small, insistent voice was asking her whether she was doing the right thing.

He had a fit about being called a sparrow, he kissed me, and then he jumped to a blond bubblehead he'd known for five seconds. Get rid of him.

She was sure. With a firm sense of purpose, she pushed open the door, only faintly hearing the tinkle of the bell.

"Welcome to Kew's Curiosity Shop," squawked the parrot, hopping from foot to foot on its perch. "Where Curiosity is our middle name."

"Yes, I remember. How are you, Henrik?" When the parrot didn't answer, just gave her a quizzical stare, Kally called out, "Mr. Kew, are you here?"

"Of course." And just like before, one minute there was empty space, and the next it was full of Mr. Kew. Today he was wearing a brocade smoking jacket and a black velvet cap. Still beaming, still twinkling, he leaned closer. "Are you enjoying Sir Crispin?"

"Do you mean the book? Or the living, breathing guy?" Kally asked sharply.

But Mr. Kew didn't answer, just kept smiling his mysterious smile.

"Mr. Kew, you *did* know what was going to happen with that book, didn't you?" She couldn't wait to hear the answer to this one. She just hoped there *were* answers. "I know you told us it was a special book. But you didn't tell us it was truly bizarre. Or what a mess it would make of our lives."

"Oh, I am sorry to hear that." But he didn't look sorry in the least.

"Life is knowing what you want, darling," the bird contributed, with an extra *bawwwwk* for emphasis.

Kally gave him a dirty look and turned to Mr. Kew. Except he was now on the other side of her. How did he do that? So she spun around and focused on the task at hand. "I know what I want, Mr. Kew. I want you to tell me how to get rid of the knights. You know, how to put them back in the book."

Tuesday groaned loudly, but Kally gave her a quelling glance. "You sold us the book, Mr. Kew. You owe us an explanation. A solution."

"Ah. You are searching for a magic spell, is that it? A magic bullet?"

"Whatever works," Kally answered as Tuesday clutched her elbow.

She whispered, "Not a bullet, Mommy! You can't shoot them. No matter what, you can't shoot them."

Mr. Kew shrugged his tiny shoulders under the thick

brocade jacket. "Life gives us many choices, many gifts." He tipped his head so far his little black hat threatened to pitch right off. "The wise woman knows when to keep and when to give back items that do not fit."

"What?" That was the best he could offer? She had two full-scale medieval knights clogging up her apartment, making a total zoo of her life, and he sounded like the Macy's Customer Service Window!

But Mr. Kew only leaned forward and patted her hand. "Don't worry, my dear. You will puzzle it all out."

"You're gonna love tomorrow," added the parrot. "I'm giving you my personal guarantee."

Kally was getting pretty tired of that bird. "So, Mr. Kew, you're saying you won't help me?"

His voice was kind and gentle when he said, "But I already have."

"I don't think—"

"Come on, Mom," Tuesday announced. "He said there's no way to, you know, ditch 'em. So we might as well go home."

Kally wasn't about to give in. "Mr. Kew?" She whirled. But he was gone. "Mr. Kew, you come out here right now and tell me what to do with those guys! This is all your fault!"

"Hey, Mommy, Septimus said he would teach me to play chess. If we go home right now maybe he can teach me before dinner."

"Dinner?" The thought of feeding those two huge men again was positively demoralizing. Kally didn't know what to think. "Mr. Kew? Are you still here?"

No answer. Not even the parrot.

Kally made a quick survey of the place, but he wasn't down any of the aisles, not in the armchair, not in any corner or cranny. "Mr. Kew, come out here!"

"Mommy, did you notice that the parrot and his cage are gone?" Tuesday asked uneasily.

What next? Was the whole bookstore going to fold up and disappear?

"I think we should leave now," her daughter whispered. "It's getting kind of creepy in here."

"Mr. Kew?" she called one last time. But there was no response, just silence in the dark, empty shop.

"Come on, Mommy." Tuesday was getting more insistent. She tugged on her mother's hand, trying to get them both to the door. "Don't worry. It'll be awesome when we keep them. I can take them for show-and-tell at play camp! Georgie brought his uncle just because he's a fireman, and this is way cooler than that."

Oh, heavens. How was she going to nip all this rampant enthusiasm in the bud? "Just because Mr. Kew didn't help us doesn't mean we can keep them."

"Mommy, this is a sign. I know we're supposed to keep them."

She allowed herself to be pulled out of the shop and up the stairs, then stopped at the top step. She cast one last glance over her shoulder at the dim bookstore window. The sign had reverted to Closed again.

Shaking her head, Kally turned away. It appeared there weren't going to be any answers at Kew's Curiosity Shop. Just plenty of curiosity.

"We can keep them, can't we?" Tuesday persisted.

She reached out and stroked her daughter's cheek. "I know you like them. And they like you, too." She considered. "Or at least Septimus seems to, what with promising to teach you to play chess. And he told you his name. Which is more than he told me."

"He *kissed* you," Tuesday said, rolling her eyes at the folly of adults. She started to troop backward down the sidewalk, not waiting for her mother. "And that means he really likes you. That's what it means on TV. So what I think is he likes you, you know, like a girlfriend, but you don't like him. And that's why you want him to go away."

"No, of course not. Tues, the main thing is that they just don't belong here." Catching up, steering Tuesday in the right direction, Kally said firmly, "You've heard of a bull in a china shop, haven't you? Well, that's kind of like the knights. Especially Crispin. Every time he turns around, I think we're going to have a hole in the wall or a foot through the floor. And Mrs. Krasselbine on our necks."

"Yes, but we could teach him how to behave. Really we could, Mommy."

"Maybe. But that's like a full-time job. And I already have a job. Which I have to go back to tomorrow morning."

Another headache. Kally lifted a hand to her forehead. She hadn't thought about work all weekend. But tomorrow was Monday, back-to-work day. On a normal weekday in June, Kally would be toiling at her desk at the Department of Immigration and Naturalization, processing citizenship applications nine to five, while Tuesday checked into summer day camp. But with magical visitors who couldn't possibly fend for themselves, alterations were going to have to be made.

She still hadn't given up hope that they might disappear on their own, of course, or that there would be some way to make them vanish in a puff of smoke. But just in case, she really ought to be making some plans.

"I can look after them while you're at work," Tuesday said excitedly. "I could take them on the subway and we could go to the Empire State Building and the Statue of Liberty and a Yankees game. Just like we did when Aunt Marena came to visit. Because they're from out of town, too."

"Tues, hold on—"

"But, Mommy, it would be so cool! And it would be okay, because it wouldn't be like I was by myself or with kids, because they're grown-ups. It's okay for me to go places with grown-ups, right?"

"Nice try. Not even close."

"But you let Daddy take me around. I know Cris is kind of goofy, but Septimus is lots more like a real adult than Daddy."

Kally narrowed her eyes. Her daughter might even be right about that one. But she wasn't giving in. "Tuesday, forget it. It's not going to happen. We're not running a tourist service. And besides, if they're still here tomorrow, I'll have to take the day off."

"Oh, goodie! Because then you can come with us to the Empire State Building and the Statue of Liberty!" Her daughter twirled around and threw her arms in the air, almost colliding with a young couple with green hair and enough rings through their body parts to start their own piercing service right there on the street. "Y'know, people don't come out of books every day. So they should get to see some stuff while they're here, shouldn't they?"

"Go for it!" the girl with the green hair called out. "Don't mess with karma, man."

Kally smiled wanly as she corralled her child and tried to get her to walk straight. "Sweetie, that isn't a good idea, even if they were staying, which they're not."

"How about a museum?" Tuesday tried. "You always like me to go to museums. It's, you know, educational. I know they'd like to see all those suits of armor at that one museum, the Met. It would make them feel at home. And then we could go to Rumpelmayer's like when Grandma comes to visit. Or the park. I really like the roller skating rink, and the castle. And the fountain with the angel."

"Tuesday," Kally interrupted, before her daughter got any further through the guidebook. "You're not taking them anywhere. I know it's kind of a shame they don't get a tour, but sweetie, think about *them*. They're different, with their clothes and the way they talk. They would feel out of place, don't you think?"

"But, Mommy, at work you get people who talk and dress different all the time, and you let *them* stay. And they're not nearly as neat as our knights."

Kally shook her head. One of these days she was going to have to find out if Tuesday planned to be a lawyer when she grew up. She was already better at arguments than a lot of the lawyers Kally ran into at the office.

She said, "Honey, those people—the ones I grant visas and citizenship applications to—are immigrants from other countries. They're not from out of books. And they're not staying at our house, where we have to feed them and hide them from Mrs. Krasselbine."

Even in the face of such sensible arguments, Tuesday wasn't giving in. She crossed her small arms over her yellow T-shirt and mumbled to herself about the Empire State Building and the Statue of Liberty.

"Listen, sweetie, you need to put that aside right away. First we have to concentrate on a solution. A permanent solution."

"Oh, no." Tuesday's shoulders slumped. "Are you still trying to banish them?"

"I'm trying to make them vanish, not banish them. And yes, of course, I am." Kally smoothed a wayward tendril of her daughter's light brown hair. "There just has to be an answer. We already looked in the book and we already asked Mr. Kew. Where else would answers be?"

Tuesday grumbled. "I don't know, and I still think they should have a real tour of New York first."

"No tours." Kally cast about for an alternative. "Do you think an exorcist would do any good?"

"I don't even know what it is," Tuesday said in an aggrieved tone. "Rosie isn't an exorcist, is she?"

"No, hon. Rosie exercises. This is exorcist, with an *O* in the middle. They're usually like priests or something, and they make evil spirits go away."

Her daughter stopped so abruptly, Kally almost tripped over her. "Tim and Cris aren't *evil!*"

"Tim? Since when is he Tim? I'm not even used to Septimus yet and you're calling him Tim now?"

Tuesday said loftily, "Septimus is too long. Tim is my friend and friends have shorter names to call each other. Like sometimes you call me Tues and Daddy calls you Kal."

"Right." Kally shook her head again. "Well, I guess you're right, and exorcising Tim isn't the best idea. Besides, we're not Catholic. So what then? A magician? They make people disappear. Or a psychic? Do they send restless spirits back where they came from?"

Tuesday didn't answer. She'd screwed up her face into a very odd expression, and she was staring at a hole in the sidewalk in front of her.

"What's up with you? Tuesday?"

They were turning the corner onto their street when Tuesday suddenly came alive. "Look, Ragamuffin is open. There's people going in. I like that store. Can we look there?"

"Ragamuffin?" It was a large, bare-bones, second-hand clothing store, taking up the second and third floors of a converted brownstone. During their married life, Brad had loved its racks and racks of cheap clothes—he got most of his wardrobe there—and he still shopped there when he came to visit. But Tuesday always whined if you so much as looked at the place. Kally cast a wary glance at her daughter. "You hate that store."

"Uh-uh. I don't hate it." She dug one toe into the sidewalk, spinning slightly.

"What's this all about? Why would you want to go to Ragamuffin all of a sudden?"

She held up pretty well under her mother's scrutiny, but she finally couldn't take it anymore. "'Cause, Mom, it's got clothes that Cris and Tim could wear, and maybe if they were dressed like normal people I could take them outside and they wouldn't stand out, you know, like bulls at a Chinese restaurant. So I thought we could get 'em some jeans or regular clothes—"

"They would still stand out, Tues. Trust me. And it's a china shop, not a Chinese restaurant. And anyway—" But she broke off as she reached their building. And suddenly it all became clear. Tuesday knew exactly what business took up the ground floor of their building, and she had tried to stage a diversion with all that stuff about Ragamuffin. "Well, will you look at that?"

"Oh, no," her daughter said mournfully.

The neon tube lights said it all. Madame Aurora Borealis, reader of auras, cards, sands and tea, past life explorer, all-around psychic counselor, was open for business. The lights were on, the pyramid and the sand dunes were visible through the big glass window, and the psychic counselor herself was puttering around in a diaphanous caftan the colors of a swirling desert sunset.

"But, Mommy, she's mean," Tuesday complained. "She has orange hair and she dresses really goofy and she doesn't like kids and she's scary when you look in her window. I don't like her. I don't think you should talk to her at all."

Kally headed down the steps to ring Aurora's door. Her fingers began to tingle as she reached for the bell.

Not again! She snatched her hand back, staring at it. Her fingers were trembling, and the tips seemed to have turned an unnatural shade of pink. This was ridiculous!

If this kept up, she'd be shaking like a leaf every time she turned a corner.

Still, she wasn't sure if this weird feeling was a good sign or a bad one. She'd felt the same sort of tingle of anticipation both times she'd visited Kew's Curiosity Shop, and looked what happened there. But maybe it meant she was on the right track, that Madame Borealis would be able to help.

"Mommy, did you change your mind?" Tuesday asked hopefully.

"No, of course not." Resolute, ignoring the omens in her fingertips, good *or* bad, Kally pressed the bell.

And nothing happened.

She pressed it again, laying on it harder and longer this time. She could hear the insistent buzz from her side, so she knew the thing was working. Peering through the glass pane in the door, she saw Aurora Borealis, plain as day, dancing around in her floating burnt-orange caftan.

The psychic counselor had her back to the door, so Kally couldn't tell what the problem was, although she had a clear enough view to note that the caftan must've been dyed to match Aurora's hair, or maybe vice versa. Kally had never seen anyone with hair—or clothing—that particular shade of wild tangerine.

So why wasn't Ms. Borealis answering? In a trance? Listening to the loud voices of messengers from above? Or just purposely ignoring the doorbell?

But if Aurora was really psychic, shouldn't she *know* people were at the door, whether she could hear the buzzer or not?

"She's not answering," Tuesday said flatly, tugging on her mother's hand. "Let's go."

"I can see her in there. She *will* answer." Kally hit the bell again. "We just have to catch her attention."

Digging in her heels, Tuesday pulled harder. "Maybe she's closed but forgot to change the sign. Maybe she doesn't like our, um, psychic vibes or something. Maybe she's a total fake and she's scared we're just the ones who'll figure her out."

With her finger still pressed to the button, Kally edged around to face her daughter. "Grasping at straws, are we?"

"No, Mom, really. It's like a sign that we're not supposed to be here."

"I don't think—"

But the door swung open abruptly, almost knocking Kally over with the scent of otherworldly potpourri and drifting incense.

Kally turned.

Madame Aurora Borealis, psychic counselor, lifted one bright orange eyebrow. Even before she spoke, Kally knew what she would say.

"You rang?"

"Maybe I'm the one with ESP," Kally muttered.

"Well? Did you want something?" the psychic asked impatiently. "The way you were buzzing my door, I figured it must be a major spiritual emergency. Poltergeist? Somebody put a curse on you?'' Her orange-red lips pursed as she gazed thoughtfully at a point over Kally's head. ''Well, your aura's in need of a major cleansing. Anyone can see that.''

''It's not my aura. It's—'' She broke off, not exactly sure how to spell this problem out. *I'm being possessed—and annoyed and attracted and driven crazy—by two guys who popped out of a book?* Instead, Kally asked, ''Can we come in?''

''You can. But not the kid.'' Aurora shrugged, rearranging the sleeve of her flowing garment, giving Tuesday a slitty glance. ''I don't allow kids. They play in my sand and disrupt the flow of my chakras. Very disturbing on a spiritual level.''

''I told you she wasn't nice,'' Tuesday whispered loudly. ''And I don't think she's psychic, either. Or she wouldn't think we were here to get our aura dusted. That is *so* wrong!''

''Cleansed, purified, distilled. Not *dusted.*'' Aurora sighed heavily, stepping into the incense as if to fortify herself against the indignity. ''And I didn't say you came to get your aura cleansed—I said it needed it.'' She tossed another glance over Kally's head. ''And it does. You've got the classic control-freak, gift-horse-in-the-mouth aura.''

''How flattering,'' Kally said tartly. ''I'm sorry we bothered you. Because as you can see, I do have a child with me. And I'm not exactly going to leave her out here on the street to fend for herself while I come in and get my fortune told.''

Aurora hissed and stiffened. ''I don't tell fortunes.

I am a registered past-life explorer and psychic counselor. I am a *healer.* Just because you're not operating on my higher plane is no reason to get insulted."

"Yeah, well, we're not staying to get healed or insulted, thank you very much." Kally turned to shoo Tuesday away from the door. It didn't take much—her daughter was already on the top step before Kally had even lifted one foot.

Behind them, Aurora Borealis moaned loudly. With one heavily ringed hand clutching the thick crystal hanging from her neck, she cried, "Endymion says *stop!* Endymion, my wise and mighty spirit guide, sends a warning—you are in deep trouble, in desperate need of my powers to assist you! You walk away at your peril. You are in the midst of a dark night of the soul, a nightmare."

Kally stilled. "Dark knight?"

In a much more normal tone of voice, Aurora said peevishly, "Yeah, dark night. That's what I said, isn't it?"

"No, Mommy, no!"

"Look, we have business to do here," Ms. Borealis snapped. "Spiritual healing takes time, you know. Besides, you live upstairs. So send the kid up by herself and get in here so we can get started."

Kally took a step toward the psychic. "How did you know we live in this building?"

Aurora shrugged again. "It's my business to know. I'm clairvoyant, remember?"

Tuesday raced over to yank her mother's hand. "She's just lucky, Mom," the child protested. "It's all made up."

"But, Tues, she mentioned the Dark Knight. Maybe she really can help us."

"It's not help. It's, like, *murder!*" Tuesday bolted up the steps to the street, then pounded up the front steps into the lobby of their apartment building.

"Tuesday?" Kally called. She ran after her daughter, hesitating only long enough to shout, "Don't go anywhere. I'll be right back," to the psychic, who didn't look any too happy about obliging.

By the time Kally raced through the lobby, past the mailboxes, rounded the corner and started up the stairs to their apartment, she could hear Tuesday's footfalls several floors above her. Huffing and puffing, Kally followed. Her daughter was getting more difficult by the moment, and she blamed those infernal knights. Tuesday was a lovely, considerate child before *they* came blasting into her life!

Kally coasted to a stop outside their door. "Tuesday? Are you in there?" she demanded, as she fiddled with her purse to look for her keys. No answer. This was getting to be a habit. And where had her keys run off to? "Tuesday Malone, open this door," she said sternly. "You know better than to run off by yourself. You are in big trouble."

The door swung open slowly, stiffly. Her nose firmly in the air, Tuesday declared, "I got you away from that horrid place, didn't I?"

"Well, as long as I know you're safe..." Kally backed up a step. "I have an appointment."

Tuesday's mouth dropped open. "You're not even going to come in and see them before you—before you..."

"If you say murder again, young lady, you will be grounded for the rest of your life." And with as much dignity as she could muster, Kally turned on her heel and went to the stairs. Behind her, she heard the door slam.

"Lock it," she called. "And put on the chain. I'll be back in a few minutes."

Still, every step down the stairs felt like a mile. Why was she so loath to do this when it had to be done? Tuesday was out of control, Crispin was an overgrown lout, and Septimus was…

Septimus.

A vision of his dark, mysterious eyes, licking her with heat and fire, filled her mind. *Oh, dear.* That was right before he'd kissed her. And it was wonderful.

She swallowed, remembering every detail. The kiss, his arms, the lean strength of his body as he held her near.

But a little voice whispered, *He's not real. He's a made-up guy, out of a book, and he doesn't have a clue how the world works. He still thinks you're disguised as a boy and imprisoned in a tower.*

His heart, his brain, the blood in his veins… They weren't real. So how could he know where he was or what he wanted?

Does he want you? Rosie? The Holy Grail?

All he knew was what some unknown author had written for him. And the way he was written, he'd go for the newest quest at hand.

Kally steeled her heart. When push came to shove, both Septimus and Cris were bound by vows, by times and experiences she could never fathom, never hope to understand. The best she could hope for was to be rid of both of them. Once that was accomplished, Tuesday would start behaving again, life would go back to normal, and…

No more Septimus.

Life would go back to normal. And she wasn't going to think any further ahead than that.

Chapter Eight

Tuesday slammed the door on her mother, turning to meet her favorite knight. "She's not the boss of me!"

Septimus raised a dark eyebrow. "You should not speak to your mother so," he said softly. "It is disrespectful, princess."

Tuesday crossed her arms over her yellow T-shirt with such an air of determination he had to work hard not to smile. "But she makes me so mad. She is so mean sometimes, like she knows everything and I don't get to decide anything. And this time, she is wrong, wrong, wrong."

Behind them, Sir Crispin shouted, "The witch seeks the dog! Beware, Dorothy!"

Tuesday rolled her eyes, and Septimus could hold back his smile no longer. Such a bright, spirited child. And so insightful to have seen the cracks in the Golden Dunderhead's armor so very quickly.

"Come, princess," he said. "Let us put our heads together to see if we can solve this impasse with your mother."

"No way," she said grumpily. "I want you guys to

stay forever. And Mommy wants you gone, like yesterday."

"I fear the Lady Kally's less than hospitable feelings must be charged to my account," he said ruefully.

Septimus admitted to himself that he should never have lost his temper, never have charged in as rash and reckless as his arch nemesis, never have tasted the sweet, honeyed lips of the enchanting Lady Kallista.

And yet he found he could not regret his actions. Not when he conjured up the memory of that kiss.

His smile widened. Lady Kally had been very angry with him. Her pretty, even features had flushed with color, her wide hazel eyes had sparkled with temper... Enchanting.

He had to admit, he fair enjoyed vexing her. Was it his fault if she happened to be even more pleasing to his eyes when she was cross?

Yes, he did enjoy seeing her blood rise. He did, indeed.

"Hey, Tim, come on," Tuesday interrupted, breaking into his reverie and pulling on his hand. "I thought we were going to put our heads together."

"But of course, princess." He sat on a marvelously comfortable chair, musing again that this new world might not be so difficult to get accustomed to. "Think you there is a way around your mother's ire?"

"I don't know. I've been trying, but I just can't come up with anything." Chewing her lip, Tuesday perched on the arm of his chair.

She tipped her head toward him, and he patted her shoulder fondly, wishing he knew how to banish the distressed expression from her small face. Such a precious child. In another place, another time, he would not have minded claiming such a child for his own.

"Princess," he began. He didn't know quite how to frame it, but there was some information he found himself most desirous of obtaining. "Princess, I took it from your lady mother's words that your father, your sire, has not departed this earthly coil."

"Huh?"

"Has your father passed on to his heavenly reward?" he asked delicately. He didn't want to cause the child any undue grief.

"Oh, dead, you mean? No, he's not dead. They're divorced. Do you know what that is?"

"Yes, of course." Divorce existed even in his vocabulary, although it was hardly something for men of honor. Kings, perhaps, who wished to be rid of inconvenient queens, might find the dissolution of their vows useful. And women whose husbands disappeared on quests and never returned. But who would wish to dissolve the bonds with the likes of Kally and Tuesday? "He has abandoned you, then?" he asked with some confusion.

"Oh, no. I mean, I still see him sometimes. He's kind of..." Tuesday rolled her eyes again. "Kind of dopey sometimes. Like he doesn't pick me up when he's supposed to. Or call when he's late or stuff. Mommy used to get sad about how he is, but now she just thinks we should be ready for him to not be there when he's supposed to and not care."

"In breaking faith with you, he dishonors himself," Septimus said darkly.

"Not really. Things are kind of different here,"

Tuesday assured him. "I like my dad. Even if he is kind of a baby."

Septimus shook his head. He could not pretend to understand. That was true of so many things in this new place, this New York, where desirable young ladies cropped their hair, donned formfitting trousers and roamed the streets of the city unaccompanied, where maidens lived shut away in tall towers whether they were enchanted or not, where small children owned books of all knowledge, neatly alphabetized from *A* to *Z*, where victuals were chilled and kept right at hand, where tiny creatures danced and sang within magical television boxes....

"So, Tim," Tuesday ventured, leaning in a little closer. "What do you think about staying? I mean, do you want to?"

"Stay or go, I am not certain it is within my purview to choose," he told her. "Would I could choose, I think..."

It might be a strange and peculiar land, but Kally and Tuesday were part of it. Even if it was not his own land, he suddenly realized he felt more welcome here than he had anywhere in his misty memory.

At Camelot, he was the last knight at the far curve of the Round Table, not Arthur's favorite, nor Guinevere's, neither.

In the eyes of the Fair Rosaminda, he was a distant second to the Golden Booby.

And even as a child, the seventh son of the cold, indifferent Lord of the Lake of Midnight, he knew well that he had been no one's favorite, a dark and moody boy, overlooked and unloved.

But here... The small princess beamed at him, and he basked in the uncomplicated warmth of a summer's day. The beautiful Lady Kally gazed at him, her honeyed eyes warm and wanting, and he felt the heat of a sultry summer's night.

In their eyes, he saw himself not as a dark lord following wicked impulses, a mere thorn in the side of the truly good. Instead, he was a man. An honorable, desirable man.

"I would fain stay," he said, surprising even himself.

"Oh, goodie. I was hoping you'd say that." Tuesday jumped up and down with excitement, clapping her small hands together. "And the first thing we should do is make you fit in better, don't you think? Like maybe different clothes?"

Before he had a chance to answer, there was a rap upon the door, and a voice he recognized as that of the Fair Rosaminda called, "Anybody home? I forgot to tell you something."

The Golden Goat vaulted from his place before the magic box, pushing aside any resistance, crying out, "Rosaminda! My one true love!" as he wrenched open the door.

"Hi, Cris. How's it hangin'?"

He blinked. "How hangs what, perchance?"

"You, silly." She giggled, batting her lashes at the Golden Imbecile.

Septimus bristled. It was always thus. The woman had been promised to him by her father, good King Alardyce. By the Hallowed Sword of Uther Pendragon, he would not stand by and watch....

"Where is my sword?" he demanded. "I shall show him, once and for all, to whom honor belongs."

But Tuesday tugged on his sleeve. "Tim, you shouldn't get upset about Rosie. She's really nice, but she's kind of a bimbo, you know," she whispered. "Maybe you should let Cris have her."

Her words stopped him in his tracks.

First, he wondered idly what a bimbo was. Nothing commendable, to be certain.

As the bimbo in question giggled again, placing her dainty fingers around the bulging arm muscle of the Golden Simpleton, Septimus found himself quite certain she was *not* the Fair Rosaminda.

"Another wicked enchantment," he muttered. "That such as she should blind my eyes. That I should see what could not be. That I should be so gulled, so deceived. It is absurd."

This was not the Fair Rosaminda. This was a common maid dressed in a jester's garb.

"Absurb," Tuesday echoed. "Right, Tim."

"Hey, you guys," Rosie called. "Me and Cris are going to go into the gym for awhile. He's feeling really, you know, cooped up here. So we're going to blow off a little steam, pump some iron. It'll be great!"

"The Fair Rosaminda calls and I must heed," Sir Crispin said happily.

And the two of them were out the door before Septimus or Tuesday could offer even so much as a word.

"Okay, well, he's taken care of," the child said with a shrug. "So here's my plan. You and me can go to this store I know and maybe get some clothes so you'll look, you know, like everybody else. Well, you won't, 'cause you're cuter than most of them, but still. Closer, you know."

"Shall we sally forth, my lady?" he asked, offering his arm. This would mark his first look at the world outside Kally's tower. And yet he felt no fear. He was Sir Septimus, a knight of the realm, defender of maidenly virtue. Nothing would hurt his young princess. Not on his watch.

As he followed young Lady Tuesday into the antechamber, he inquired, "Think you there is a chance your mother will hold my form in higher esteem when I return garbed more in the current mode?"

"You mean, will she like you better if you're dressed more normal?"

He curved his lips into a dark smile. "Exactly."

Tuesday grinned at him, and he realized again how much he liked this saucy child. She said, "It's worth a shot."

"Worth a shot." He stored this new phrase.

Worth a shot. To bring a light of admiration to Kally's eyes, it was indeed.

AURORA WAS WAITING by the door when Kally arrived. Sweeping inside, the psychic strode right past the big sand dune and the rather awkward-looking pyramid, pulling her new client along to the back of the room.

Kally tried not to gawk. So far, the place was a little strange, but nothing she couldn't handle. Around her, the room's surfaces were stark white, except for a deep orange splash that curved across the floor, up onto the walls and even the ceiling. It made the place seem round, off-balance, and made Kally a little dizzy.

At the very back of the room, under a gauzy white canopy of some sort, Aurora motioned for Kally to sit on a round white rug in front of a small table. The table held a stack of worn cards, a rather frail teacup with sludge in the bottom, and a candle that smelled strongly of vanilla.

Kally was quite disappointed. She was going to need more than some warped cards and a dirty teacup to get her out of this pickle.

"Place yourself inside the circle, please. I sense you are in need of my strongest spiritual concentration and cleansing powers." Ms. Borealis closed her eyes, lifted her chin and pushed back her mane of tangerine hair. Throwing her arms skyward, she announced, "I'm ready to begin."

And then she tossed herself onto the floor and sat cross-legged on a fat pillow on the other side of the table.

"Well? Are you going to sit so we can get started?"

"Oh, sure." Kally scrambled to find a comfortable way to sit on the little rug.

"You must be completely inside the circle. And be very still," her new spiritual adviser ordered. "Very, very still."

Kally stuck one leg underneath her, then switched to the other. She was fairly tall, and there just wasn't any way to get all of herself onto the rug. She glanced around, dubious. "Does this really help?"

"Of course it helps," Ms. Borealis snapped. "Would I ask you to do it if it didn't? Now sit there and be quiet so I can contact Endymion, my spirit guide, and unleash my powers."

"Okay, okay."

Dutifully, Kally crouched in the center of her rug, feeling like a kindergartner at nap time. She hugged her knees to her chest, watching for any signs of life from her psychic counselor, who had closed her eyes and tipped back her head. Aurora Borealis looked for all the world as if she were going to sleep.

Kally tried to be patient. But while Aurora dozed—if that was what she was doing—Kally couldn't help but worry about the apartment full of stir-crazy fighting men upstairs. Stir-crazy fighting men and one small child who had probably spirited the whole group onto the subway and out to the Bronx by now.

She leaned forward, bracing her elbows on the small table. "Excuse me," she said, "but would it help if I told you what the problem was? Kind of, you know, cut to the chase?"

Aurora pried open one eye. "Wouldn't I have asked you if I thought it would help?" she asked angrily. "You are really messing with my vibes, I hope you know that. And get your elbows off my divining table."

"Sorry."

Sitting back, Kally sighed, watching as Aurora lapsed into snooze mode. The chances of finding help here began to seem as remote as the North Pole. She waited another second or two, glancing anxiously at the clock over Aurora's head. Finally, she just couldn't wait. Who knew what was happening upstairs by now?

"Excuse me," she repeated, leaning forward onto

the table again, accidentally knocking the stack of cards and sending one onto the floor. "Oops. Sorry. I didn't mean to—"

"Oh, yes!" Aurora cried, pouncing on the card and holding it aloft. "I knew I'd get a sign. The Knight of Swords."

"The Knight of Swords?" Kally paled. That sounded on target. Maybe there was something to this.

"This indicates," her spiritual counselor continued, "that there is much movement in your life. Especially men. Dashing, virile men. Coming and going."

"Well, coming, anyway," Kally agreed. "But it's the going I'm interested in right now."

Aurora bent near the table, poring over her cards. "Hmm. This is very interesting."

"You mean you can tell what my problem is from there?"

"Well, actually, no." She frowned at Kally as she settled onto her pillow. "I'm having trouble getting through the protective layers around your higher mind and your inner energy. You are one tightly wrapped enchilada."

Kally wondered whether that was good or bad. "So should I tell you what the problem is?"

The frown deepened. "You'd better."

Where to begin? It wasn't like this was something she wanted to admit she actually believed. But she was speaking to a past-life explorer and psychic counselor. If anyone would understand fictional phenomena showing up in your living room, it ought to be Aurora Borealis.

Kally began at the beginning. "Well, my daughter,

the one who was here before, got this book at this little store down the street, Kew's Curiosity Shop. Have you ever seen it?"

"No," Ms. Borealis returned quickly. She didn't look pleased. "Is this going to be like a monkey's paw story or something? Gremlins, that kind of thing? Because I don't have time for people pitching screenplay ideas. Been there, done that."

Kally blinked. "This is no screenplay, I assure you. Who would make up something like this?"

"You'd be surprised. Never mind. Go on."

"Right." She picked up her story where she'd left off. "So Tuesday bought this book about knights, like Round Table knights, you know? Gawain, Lancelot, that kind of thing, only this was Sir Crispin, the Golden Knight of Yore, and his nemesis, Sir Septimus, the Dark Knight. I read the book, too, and I fell asleep reading it." She could sense Aurora growing restless, so she got to the good part. "And the first thing I knew they were right there, in front of me, in their armor, with their swords, fighting. Like a joust or something, in my living room. They slashed my sofa bed!"

"Uh-huh. So, what then? King Arthur and his pal Lance are still in your living room?" Under her wild mop of tangerine hair, Aurora's eyes glinted with disbelief.

"No, not King Arthur. Sir Crispin and the Dark Knight." Kally started to rise. "Look, if you don't believe me, I can save us both some time. I thought you could help me, but I guess you're not interested."

Aurora chewed the tangerine gloss off her bottom

lip. "I'm interested. But you're sure this isn't a setup, '60 Minutes' or something?"

"I'm sure," Kally offered glumly. "You know, if you want to, if it would help, you can come upstairs and meet the big lugs yourself. We've got armor, swords, even the book if you need proof."

"I don't think that will be necessary." Aurora waved Kally to a sitting position. She bent closer and added in a conspiratorial undertone, "I can't believe it myself, but your story explains a lot of things in your aura and the cards. And the general spiritual projections. Endymion kept shouting at me about dark knights, but I thought it was the usual mumbo jumbo. Night, you know. Dark journey, nothing to fear but fear itself, you know. But now that I get it, this really clears things up."

"So what do I do?"

"I don't know yet." She scratched her chin thoughtfully. "It's not exactly like poltergeists or ghosts, although in a way... Angelic or other celestial manifestation? No. Although I did see this play where the guy had to wrestle an angel to get it to go away. But still, more like a genie from a bottle, isn't it? Wonder what they do when they want the genie back in the bottle?"

Kally waited. "I don't know. Do you?"

"Let me look at the books." Her caftan trailing, Aurora hiked herself off the pillow and slid out of view behind a door. "Give me a minute."

"I don't have a minute!" Kally called after her. But she waited anyway.

Finally, when she had all but given up hope, the

past-life explorer returned carrying a large, dusty volume and a feather. She appeared to be studying one specific page as she swept into the room. "Hmm... Okay, that might work."

"What?" Kally demanded, trying to get close enough to make out some of the words. She could see the chapter heading, something about banishment of otherworldly forces and spirit projections.

How odd that a feeling of dread seemed to settle in the pit of her stomach. So Tuesday had been right—they were going to banish the knights. Right now? Could she delay the spell long enough to run upstairs and say goodbye?

"What does it say?" she asked anxiously. "And what does the feather do?"

Aurora looked up. "It's a bookmark."

"Oh. Sorry."

"Calm down, will you? I've got the enchantment right here." She narrowed her gaze. "It's a hundred dollars, up front. This isn't really my area of expertise, so I can't be responsible if it doesn't work. No guarantees, you understand?"

A hundred dollars? With no guarantee it would even work? Kally winced. She was crazy to trust a charlatan like Aurora. But what choice did she have? "Do you take credit cards?"

"MasterCard, Visa, American Express." Holding the book at eye level, Aurora advised, "At noon tomorrow, make sure both the knights and the book are in the bathroom in your apartment."

Her first thought was that she'd have till noon. And

her second... "The bathroom? What's that got to do with anything?"

"I have to send the spell up the plumbing." The spiritualist lifted her hands. "It's the only way."

"The plumbing? You're kidding, right?" This was getting too ridiculous for words. She might as well throw her hundred dollars out the window.

"What choice do you have?" Aurora asked stiffly. "Do you want to be rid of these boys or not?"

Kally considered. Order would be restored. No noise, no confusion, no kisses in the kitchen... "Yes," she said quietly. "Yes, I do."

"All right. So get them in the bathroom at noon with the book." She gazed at her book. "I'll need to study up before then. Let's just run that credit card, shall we? Oh, and one last thing. You and your kid should stay out of the bathroom while this is going on." Ms. Borealis raised a thin orange eyebrow. "Or you might end up stuck in the book with them."

Kally paused. That was a new wrinkle she didn't even want to think about. "Um, okay. Thanks for the warning."

But deep down, she still couldn't quite believe her life had been reduced to this.

"HELLO? Tuesday, where are you?"

No answer.

No knights, no little girl. Just an empty apartment full of swords and armor.

There were several messages on the answering machine, but they were all from Brad, sounding very cranky and professing to be worried about his daughter and whatever was going on with Kally and her "stripper friends."

She didn't need to think about that right now. Brad and his idiotic suspicions could be dealt with. Once the knights were gone and peace was restored, Brad would be a piece of cake. But not right now.

Right now she had to figure out where they were. And come up with some way to get both knights and the book in the bathroom by noon. Exactly noon. High noon.

And not before.

Kally swallowed. What if Aurora did a practice spell while she was on her way up the stairs. What if...

"It's probably just that Tuesday called a cab and took them to Yankee Stadium or the Statue of Liberty. I'm sure they didn't all disappear into the book. I'm sure. I mean, the armor's here. They would've taken their armor if they went back, wouldn't they?"

She cursed stupid Aurora Borealis for putting that idea into her head. She ran into the bedroom, found the book and checked to make sure Tuesday wasn't there on the pages. No Tuesday. Thank goodness. Although she could have sworn the thing was different.

"Now it's calling him Sir Septimus some of the time instead of just the Dark Knight. He's got a name," she said. "And his face is here more, too."

She must be mistaken. The book couldn't change, could it?

"Well, if it can spit out full-grown knights, why not change every once in awhile, just for fun?"

Kally set the book on the floor in the bathroom and

threw a towel on top of it, getting ready for tomorrow. But her knees were shaking as she walked into the living room to sit on the sofa and wait for Tuesday. Who cared about tomorrow? She was scared to death about her daughter.

Alone on the streets of New York with two irresponsible, short-tempered, illegal aliens.

Should she call Brad? The police?

"Tuesday, the least you could've done was leave a note," she shouted to the walls of the apartment.

She noted idly that the video was still in the VCR. Did that mean they'd watched it or not? Did it matter?

"She's just out seeing the sights," Kally told herself. "She'll be back as soon as they wait in that godawful line to go to the top of the Empire State Building."

But what if Tuesday had decided to run away, to hide the knights somewhere to save them from extinction? Kally was ready to kill her daughter, except she was too worried to even think about it.

And Septimus. He'd done that nifty vow, all sincere and charming, and then let her precious child walk out into the big, bad world, without even leaving a note. What a terrible way to behave. Crispin, she would have expected, but not Septimus.

"I'm going to kill him, too. Just please let him come back long enough to do it!"

She was reaching for the phone, ready to call Brad and face his wrath but at least get him in on the search, when she heard the doorknob turn.

She leaped to her feet, dropping the phone with a clatter. The first thing she saw was a familiar head of light brown hair, just a shade lighter than cinnamon, with a few streaks of gold.

"Tuesday," she cried, her voice full of relief and anxiety all at once. "Where have you..."

But her voice died out when she saw what—who—was behind her little girl. A man. Septimus. But not Septimus.

Tall and dark, his long, thick, mahogany hair flowing over his shoulders, his eyes wary and deep, he definitely looked like the Septimus she knew. But he was wearing black jeans and a T-shirt. The Dark Knight, in jeans?

"Septimus?" she asked slowly. "What happened? Where did you get those clothes?"

He held out his arms. "They are rather comfortable, actually. And I noted, out on the streets of this bizarre city of yours, that I do not look untoward. Although the maids I passed seemed quite admiring, no one seemed to notice that I didn't belong." He grinned. "Nobody called the cops."

"Told you, Mommy." Tuesday pranced into the room with a very smug look on her young face. "I took him to Ragamuffin and we got him and Cris some clothes. And now he's not a bull in a Chinese restaurant anymore, is he?"

"Bull in a china shop," she said automatically. "And that was Crispin. But that can wait. You have some explaining to do, young lady. Leaving without my permission. Against my express orders! And not even a note."

Kally shook her head, doing her best to look mean and forbidding. It wasn't easy when all she wanted to do was scoop up Tuesday and hug the stuffing out of her. And then try Septimus on for size.

Okay, so he was gorgeous before in his knight clothes. But now he looked so…real. As if he weren't a figment of somebody's imagination or a runaway from Medieval Land but a real, live guy. A little too moody and dangerous to be good for you. But the kind of man who could definitely sweep a woman off her feet.

Standing there, gazing at him, Kally couldn't help feeling nervous. How would she handle this new Septimus, this I-look-like-someone-who-could-escort-a-supermodel-to-Planet-Hollywood Septimus?

Very, very carefully.

Chapter Nine

Kally focused on her wayward daughter for the time being. "Tuesday, you are in serious trouble. Go to your room."

But if she sent her daughter to her room, then she'd be alone with Septimus.

"No, wait. I want to talk to you first." And then she realized. Alone with the Dark Knight? "Where the heck is Sir Crispin?"

Tuesday rolled her eyes. "Rosie came by right after you left, and Cris went with her. I think Septimus, um, Tim would've like dueled him or something, but since you made him promise not to, he just stayed with me."

"That was nice." She tried to send him a glance without actually looking at him. But failed. She saw. He noticed and cocked an eyebrow as if to ask, *Like what you see?*

Oh, yeah.

"So then," Tuesday went on, getting more animated, completely missing the undercurrents in the room, "I thought about Ragamuffin and how you might change your mind if you saw how regular and normal Tim and Cris could look. So me and Tim went over to the store and this is what we got.''

Septimus dutifully waved a brown paper sack. He pulled out a couple of dark T-shirts and another pair of jeans for her inspection. And the bag was still full.

Kally was astonished. ''Where did you get the money for that? Rob a bank? Mug some guy by threatening him with your sword?'' And then another catastrophe hit her. ''Has Crispin been with Rosie all this time? Don't you think he's going to tell her the whole thing and she'll start screaming for the guys in the white coats and we'll all be in the loony bin before dinner? Arrested or hauled off to Bellevue, which is worse?''

Tuesday blinked. She wasn't used to seeing her mother hysterical. ''Um, no. I don't think Rosie will care.'' She paused. ''Okay, so about the money. We used my birthday money from Grandma. Plus Septimus took his busted helmet to the pawn shop down the street and the guy said it was solid silver and gave him lots of cash, didn't he, Tim?''

''I have no standard of comparison,'' Septimus said ruefully. ''I've never seen coin that is not coin, not even metal. Of what value is paper?'' He shook his head. ''And yet, this fondness for green paper is no stranger than anything else about your New York. I tried not to stop and stare so as not to endanger the young princess, but this place is passing odd.''

''Septimus, you walked the streets of New York. You left the, uh, castle. And all you can say is that it's passing odd?''

He shrugged. But there was a glint of humor in

those obsidian eyes. "When you find yourself adrift in a new world, as I have found myself, you learn quickly to celebrate a certain adaptability. So, to echo a young fellow I observed out on those streets you spoke of, I plan to keep my nose clean and stay out of trouble."

If she hadn't been so emotionally fragile at that moment, she might've laughed.

"You are amazing," she murmured. "Somehow, I doubt Crispin fared as well."

"Oh, I'm sure he did fine, Mom." Tuesday chewed on the end of her hair. "Rosie told us she was taking him to lift weights at her health club. So I figure he got to show off his muscles and act like a cool dude, and that's all he cares about, don't you think?"

Kally's mouth fell open. "Well, Tuesday, you're amazing, too. And I think you've hit Crispin's nail on the head."

"His nail? Or his mail?" Septimus queried.

"I'll tell you later." Kally crossed to her daughter. "Listen, Tues, I'm still really mad at you. And you will be punished. Trust me. But later. Right now..." She bent and hugged her, hard. "I was so worried about you."

"Aw, Mom. I was with Tim. There wasn't anything to worry about." But she hugged her mother, nonetheless. "Think about it, Mommy. Tim's slewed dragons and rescued maidens and all that good stuff. He can handle one little walk to the pawn shop and Ragamuffin."

"Okay. For now."

When someone began to pound on the door, Kally

wasn't sure what to think. Brad, still fussing about male strippers? Mrs. Krasselbine, on the scent of unapproved overnight guests? Or someone even worse?

Could her life get any worse?

She avoided the door, tossing herself carelessly in a comfy chair. "You answer," she told Tuesday. "I'm having a bad day and I just don't have enough left to even see who it is."

"Mommy, you never let me answer the door." Tuesday made a funny face and came closer, peering at her mother. "Are you sure you're okay?"

Kally put her hand over her forehead. "I haven't got a clue."

"Why don't I take care of it?" Septimus inquired tactfully, already moving to the door. "I seem to be the best equipped to welcome visitors at this moment in time."

"You're sounding more and more like a regular guy all the time," Kally mused. Except that a regular guy wouldn't rouse himself to go to the door. Certainly not her ex-husband, anyway. "Wait." She shot up in her chair. "You can't answer the door. What if it's Brad?"

But Septimus smiled. "Think you I am afraid of one small weasel of an ex-husband? I can deal with your Brad."

"Tuesday!" Kally rounded on her daughter. "What exactly did you tell him about your father?"

"I didn't say hardly anything," the child protested.

"She didn't need to," Septimus added darkly. "What else can I think of a man who deserts such a beautiful and true wife and child, leaving them to fend for themselves in this cruel world?''

She thought she appreciated the sentiment. She wasn't sure. Because all she really heard was the word *beautiful.*

He thought she was beautiful?

Kally couldn't help the small smile hovering around her lips. He thought she was beautiful. And he was willing to throttle her ex-husband because of it.

But when he swung open the door, it was only Rosie and Crispin waiting.

''Jeepers, it took you long enough,'' Rosie said cheerfully. ''You guys playing a game or something?''

''Discussing matters of import,'' Septimus returned coolly.

Kally was keeping her eye on him. Was he still pursuing Rosie as the answer to a knight errant's dream? Or had he woken up and smelled the coffee? She already knew Septimus was smart enough not to be fooled by the likes of Rosie. But his vows and his code and all that stuff seriously complicated things. If he really believed his sacred knightly oaths bound him to Rosie, it wouldn't matter if he thought she was as appealing as an eel.

Septimus was a man of honor. And he'd stick like glue.

Kally watched him watch Rosie, and she wished she'd just come right out and asked him if he still thought the dim bulb aerobics instructor was the Fair Rosaminda.

''Discussing? Huh. That sounds boring.'' Rosie

beamed at Sir Crispin, who trailed her, carrying what appeared to be her exercise bag.

Kally's eyes widened. Cris was decked out in tights and a tank top, both in muscle-baring Lycra, in a rainbow of bright blues and purples. It was an eye-popping outfit, in a tasteless sort of way.

"Don't you think that sounds boring, Cris?" Rosie prompted. "People like us go more for the physical stuff, don't you think?"

"Assuredly." Tossing his golden locks over one shoulder, Sir Crispin strutted into the room like a peacock, and no wonder, in that getup.

"Hey, Cris," Tuesday interjected, "we went to Ragamuffin and got some new clothes, so you guys would fit in better here. Want to see? We got you some jeans and T-shirts, like Septimus and my mom are wearing."

Crispin gave their clothes a gander. "The Golden Knight, sporting the feathers of the plainest moldy wren? Fie on't!" he bellowed. "Rags may be good enough for such a lowly fellow as the Dark Knight. But never shall rags adorn a personage such as myself. Why, the royal house of Glinn calls me its own. Should I dishonor my fathers by appearing in such rude attire? Never, do you hear?"

He changed his tone and swung his arms wide. "You have but to cast your eyes upon the splendid garments spun for me by the dainty hands of the Fair Rosaminda to gainsay what I needs must wear."

"Does he think Rosie made that stuff?" Tuesday whispered to her mother. "She gets it from the lost and found at the gym. Even I know that."

"Shh." Kally wanted to hear what would come next from the lips of the Golden Dunderhead.

"This attire," he said, running a hand over his manly chest, "befits a glorious knight with so many astounding feats to his credit. And yet you would cloak me in peasant garb? Why, you must be mad."

"Oh, we're getting there," Kally muttered. She turned to Rosie. "So, did you guys have fun?"

"Yeah, we had a blast!" Rosie said enthusiastically. "I showed Cris how to use the Nautilus machines, and he took to them real well. Man alive, can he bench-press. And then we hit the bikes, we did spinning." She thumped him on one massive bicep. "This big guy has stamina to burn."

"The Fair Rosaminda has helped me stoke up a mighty appetite," Crispin roared, heading for the kitchen. "I would fain eat the Great Ogre of Charlevoix *and* his giant boar!"

"Don't you just love the way he talks?" Rosie giggled.

"Not really. Not when he's expecting me to feed him."

Kally was getting closer by the minute to tossing the big oaf onto the street. If there was only some way to convince him to forget her name and address...

She reminded herself that she had at least a chance of getting rid of him tomorrow in the bathroom with the book. What to do about Septimus was more complicated, since he was assimilating rather nicely. But Crispin was getting on her nerves.

"Yeah," Rosie told her with another giggle. "I already fed him a couple of times but he wasn't real crazy about eating vegetarian like I do. When it came time for a real meal, he wanted to come back here pronto. Something about viands. I told him, I've heard of veal, but viands goes right over my head. You know what that is?''

''No, as a matter of fact I don't. But he's not getting it, whatever it is.''

''Mommy,'' Tuesday said logically, ''if you don't feed him, he'll just be running off with Rosie all the time. So I think maybe you better make him his viands or whatever if you want him to stick around.''

''Why would I...''

She already knew the answer. If Crispin was out running around with Rosie, somebody was bound to start asking questions about where he came from and how he got there. Which could only mean trouble.

But if he stuck around in the apartment until noon tomorrow, she had a shot at sending him back where he belonged.

Until noon tomorrow. Surely she could live with the Golden Dingdong that long. *If* she could scrape together enough cash to pay for dinner. What did you feed someone who wanted great ogre with a side order of giant boar?

She smiled wanly. ''Tuesday, do you have any of your birthday money from Grandma left? The only thing I can think of is to order lots and lots of pizza.''

But her daughter screwed up her face. ''I only have three dollars.''

Wordlessly, Septimus stepped forward. He reached into his pocket and pulled out a fifty-dollar bill. ''Pardon, Lady Kally. Will this help? It appears to be of a larger denomination. Is this what a proper meal fetches?"

"I don't know about proper, but that ought to cover a few pizzas."

She gave him a wide smile as she walked over to get the money. But when she moved to pluck the bill from his hand, she saw something odd flicker in his eyes. "Septimus?" she asked. "Is something wrong?"

He murmured, "Not at all. You have a very lovely smile, m'lady. Gazing at you, I felt as if I had rescued a fair damsel from the jaws of a dragon, after all. It is a most gratifying feeling."

He held out the bill, still gazing at her with that peculiar intensity, and she grabbed it and whirled before she had a chance to think about any of this too deeply.

You have a very lovely smile, m'lady.

As she dialed the pizzeria down the street, she couldn't help thinking how handy Septimus was making himself, what with dishing out soft compliments, acting as her protector, charming her child, kicking in the bucks for dinner....

She let her gaze trace the length of his black-denim-clad legs, so long and strong, the lean, muscled expanse of chest under the black T-shirt, even his strong jaw.

Oh, yeah. Septimus was fine to have around.

Dangerous thoughts. Especially since she was planning to banish him tomorrow. At high noon.

KALLY SPENT a restless night, tossing and turning, muttering to herself, "Should I go through with it?

Can I? Can I not?''

Until Tuesday finally sat up and howled, ''Mommy, will you please be quiet so I can sleep? I'm going to take Septimus to Coney Island tomorrow and I don't want to be tired and cranky.''

''You're not taking Septimus anywhere tomorrow,'' Kally returned sharply. ''I have plans for both him and Cris. Tomorrow. Noon.''

Tuesday's eyes widened. ''Plans? You're still trying to get rid of them, aren't you? That Aurora woman told you something to do at noon tomorrow. How could you?''

''They don't belong here. We can't keep them. We can't afford them.'' Kally propped herself on one elbow so she could see her daughter better in the dim light. ''Besides, don't you think they'd be happier where they can slay dragons and rescue maidens and do all that fun stuff?''

''No. I asked Septimus where he'd rather be, and he said he wanted to stay here. And I think he should.'' She moved under the blanket, turning her back to her mother. But then she glanced over her shoulder. ''So how does it work, this banishing thing?''

Kally wasn't born yesterday. She knew very well that if she told Tuesday what she was planning, Tuesday would do her best to sabotage it. She wished she hadn't mentioned that it was at noon. That was bad enough.

''It's nothing for you to worry about.''

Tuesday made a harrumph sound and hid under her hair and her covers.

"Listen to me, Tuesday. You are already in the doghouse because of your little unapproved trip this afternoon. Don't push your luck. You behave, you hear me? I am the adult here, and I make the rules. Have you got that?"

There was no answer.

"Want to go visit Grandma and Great-Aunt Fannie in Florida for the rest of the summer? It can be arranged."

Tuesday shot up. "Mom! You wouldn't!"

"Don't tempt me."

"But when Daddy left us, you said it would be you and me, together, forever, for sure." Tuesday blinked, fluttering her long sandy lashes. "Are you going back on that, Mommy?"

"No, of course not." She hugged her daughter tight. Tuesday knew very well how to punch her mother's buttons, but Kally still wasn't going to be sidetracked. With Aurora Borealis's warning uppermost in her mind, she adopted a firm tone. "I want you to promise me you'll stay away from the knights tomorrow at noon. This is very serious. Promise me, Tuesday."

She looked very sulky, but she mumbled, "I promise."

"If you try to interfere, Tues, it will be like no TV for months and months, no treats, no new bears, no friends over. The worst you can think of. I'm not kidding."

She hoped the threat was severe enough to keep Tuesday from interfering. Because she just couldn't take this anymore. She couldn't sleep, couldn't work, couldn't control her daughter, couldn't control her traitorous feelings for a stupid imaginary man!

It had to stop.

THE MORNING did nothing to change her plans.

She knew most of it was just that she was exhausted. But still...

The first thing she did was call in sick so they knew not to expect her at the office. She got the distinct feeling her boss didn't believe her.

Meanwhile, Tuesday was morose and uncooperative and refused to speak to anyone except Septimus. Kally told her to get dressed for day camp, but she burst into tears. Trembling with indignation, Tuesday said, "You can't make me go away! Not now!" And rather than stage a battle royal, Kally wimped out and let her stay home.

And then Cris was starving again, and operating on way too much adrenaline. When the toaster popped unexpectedly, he skewered the poor thing with his sword!

She supposed he was lucky he wasn't electrocuted, but her toaster was a goner. Which meant they all had to eat toast from the oven. Which came out charred and black, although Crispin didn't notice as he wolfed down piece after piece.

And then she got a call from Mrs. Krasselbine's son, who told her he'd had complaints about noise from her apartment.

And another message from Brad, who sounded even more peeved this time.

All of that wasn't the worst of it, though.

Because every time she turned around, Septimus was there, watching her, giving her those moody, bittersweet glances, making her feel all jittery. She knocked over a mug full of hot coffee, dropped a knife with jelly on it and flipped half a scrambled egg out of the pan and behind the stove.

It had to stop.

As the clock ticked off the minutes till noon, Kally was a nervous wreck. Her mind flitted from wondering whether this bathroom rendezvous had a prayer of working to whether she even wanted it to work.

Was she a horrible person for wanting things the way they were, when life was peaceful and normal and dull?

Was she doing the right thing?

If she felt like this much of a louse, how could it be the right thing? And yet, the mere thought of keeping them, when they so clearly didn't belong, couldn't be right, either.

Even if I wanted him, I couldn't have him, because he's not real.

But why did he look so real? And feel so real? And why did he make her feel alive, like she hadn't felt in years?

It had to stop.

She couldn't even look at Septimus. Every time he tried to be nice or strike up a conversation, she practically ran from the room. Tuesday's accusing eyes didn't help anything.

By eleven-thirty she thought she would jump out of her skin.

When she tripped over the pile of armor in the living room, she suddenly wondered whether she was supposed to send them back dressed the way they came. What if they fell into their magic forest unarmored and unprotected? Would some wandering cyclops or sea serpent eat them for breakfast?

"Septimus! Crispin!" she called. "I need you to put on your armor. Right now."

"Why?" Septimus asked dryly. He was playing Candyland with—and keeping a watchful eye on—Tuesday, and he seemed in no hurry to jump up and start arming himself.

"Has the crone returned?" Crispin demanded. He buckled on his chest plates and grabbed his sword. "I'll run the old witch through!"

"Um, yes, that's it." Kally decided to run with his lead. "Mrs. Krasselbine just called, and she's coming up, so you have to pretend to be suits of armor again. Now."

"I heard no ring from the telephone," Septimus noted.

"It rang."

"I heard no ring."

"Me, neither." Tuesday sniffed.

"It rang," Kally repeated, louder. "Would you put on your armor, please?"

"I have no helm. I pawned it," Septimus reminded her.

"Well, put on what you have, okay?"

"But it will hardly prove a disguise if my head is visible."

"Put it on," she ordered. "Don't argue with me."

He raised a dark eyebrow, but he rose lazily from the table. "As you wish, m'lady."

Tuesday took a look at the clock and clearly knew what was up, because she burst into tears and launched herself headfirst onto the sofa.

Septimus stopped where he was. "Can you tell me what ails the young princess this morning? Something is clearly wrong, and yet she will tell me naught."

"She's just moody."

"As are you," he noted darkly. He, too, buckled on his chest and back plates, but that was as far as he went.

"What are you waiting for?" she asked them both. "There's a whole pile of tin there you haven't even touched."

"We were not prepared, so we are not attired in the proper arming doublets," Septimus told her. When she threw up her hands, he explained, "The tunic with the strings on it."

"Oh. Well, it doesn't matter." She was starting to panic as the clock edged closer to noon. "Now I need you to go into the bathroom and wait."

The Dark Knight let a long pause hang in the air. "And why, pray tell?"

"Haven't you ever heard of hiding?"

"A knight may not hide from danger," Crispin interjected grandly. "A knight of the realm may never shrink from adventure, no matter how daring."

"It's in the vows," Septimus added.

"Vows be damned—get in the bathroom!"

She took Septimus by the hand and tried to drag him, pushing Cris with a hand to the middle of his back. He was like a tree trunk, but he allowed himself to be prodded.

When the two of them saw the small space they were supposed to occupy, neither one looked pleased.

"Nay," said the Golden Knight. "I shall not tarry here with my mortal enemy but a breath away."

"I'm the damsel in distress here, and I say you will," Kally ordered.

Still grumbling, Crispin sat on the toilet. He seemed mollified when he noticed Tuesday's goldfish swimming in its little bowl on the back of the tank. "Ah," he cried, watching it swim round and round. "It is the color of the sun as it shines on the Golden Castle of Glinn!"

Kally bit her lip, trying to keep a lid on her growing unease. Looking at Cris in his psychedelic spandex with a breastplate strapped over it, she wondered, not for the first time, what the heck she thought she was doing. He was going to make quite an impact in the book in that outfit.

The book. Surreptitiously, she tapped her foot on the rug to make sure the book was still there. It was. The knights, the book and almost noon. Three minutes to go, according to her watch.

She could barely breathe with the tension that seemed to clog her throat and constrict her lungs. But it was almost over.

"You guys stay here, do you hear me? Do not leave this bathroom until I tell you it's okay to leave."

As she turned to go, Septimus reached for her hand, pulling her back. His gaze was narrow and dark. "Is this it, then?"

"I don't know," she said honestly, but her voice was no more than a whisper.

He nodded, so slightly she might not have noticed if he hadn't been so very close. "Never let it be said that I do not abide by the wishes of my lady."

All she could see was his dark, deep gaze as she backed away and shut the door.

My lady. No man had ever called her his lady before.

She had to be away from there. She felt like running into the path of the nearest bus. Instead, she scrambled into the kitchen and gripped the sink. But this was where he'd kissed her. This was no good!

Desperate to be farther away, she bolted into Tuesday's bedroom and shut the door. She squeezed her eyes shut, expecting the worst. What would happen? Would there be a cue, a clue? Maybe a bolt of lightning or a power surge?

The seconds ticked away on Tuesday's Cinderella clock. The fairy godmother's wand edged closer to noon.

Kally felt like screaming.

And then someone did. It was a decidedly male scream, more like a roar.

She jumped to her feet.

"What evil enchantment is this?" someone bellowed. Sir Crispin.

Kally ran for the door.

Chapter Ten

The door to the bathroom was wide open.

"Gone," Kally whispered. She dropped to the edge of the bathtub, gazing around her. She felt as cold and empty as the dim little room. "It worked."

The small bathroom was clean as a whistle. No knights. Except for *Sir Crispin, the Golden Knight of Yore,* which was on the floor all by itself. Kally grabbed the book, fingering the cover, noting that the corner had become singed when whatever happened happened.

Singed? Her heart leaped into her throat. Singed? What if Septimus were singed, too? If even one gorgeous hair on his head were hurt, she would never forgive herself.

What had she done?

"Oh, Septimus, I'm so sorry!"

She flipped open the cover of the book, hoping, praying, to find some sign that Cris and Septimus were now safely back in its pages where they belonged, happily jousting and carousing and slashing swords. But she hadn't even gotten past the title page when she heard high-pitched, childish laughter coming from the living room. Tuesday's voice, laughing? At a time like this?

Still clutching the book, Kally eased around the corner and into the living room. Her mouth dropped open.

All three of them—Septimus, Cris and Tuesday—were sprawled in front of the television set, watching a cartoon.

Kally's heart seemed to catch in her chest. He looked just fine. *Fine.*

He stood behind the others, and he seemed to sense her presence before they did. He turned, greeting Kally with a sardonic not-quite smile.

She was filled with incredible relief and joy. He was okay, he was in one piece, he wasn't some sea serpent's dinner.

Just for the moment, she was going to enjoy looking at him.

But the sound of Tuesday hooting with laughter broke the misty mood. She was laughing so hard she looked like she might fall down, while Sir Crispin did his best to wedge his sword into a small sliver of space around the on-off button, presumably so he could skewer the cartoon dragon cavorting on the screen.

"An evil enchantment!" he cried again, looking very frustrated and enraged. "The dragon mocks me."

Actually, the little red dragon was singing a jolly tune about the joys and difficulties of having fire breath—Kally had seen this video about a hundred times—but she could see how that might look like mocking to Crispin. Kally was too mentally exhausted, too relieved, too upset, to point out the difference.

"Hi, Mommy," Tuesday said cheerfully. Her small,

heart-shaped face was as smug as smug can be. "We're watching my Blazer the Dragon video. As soon as he saw Blazer, Cris got all scared. Even when I was little, I didn't get scared by *Blazer!*"

Kally didn't know whether to laugh or cry. "So you enticed them out of the bathroom with a cartoon dragon?"

"I don't know what that means." Tuesday glanced at the ceiling and squirmed a little. "I just put in the video and then told 'em there was a dragon in the living room. Which, you know, is true."

"Uh-huh." She paused. "Tuesday, do you know the word *sabotage?*"

The child professed ignorance, so Kally sent her off to look it up in the dictionary. But Tuesday came back on the double, sans dictionary, breathlessly reporting that the goldfish was missing from the bathroom. "There's just a little puddle where Ginger's bowl used to be!"

Kally gulped. "Then it did work." She sat with a thud, realizing how close they'd been. "It *did* work."

"What did, Mommy?"

"The banishing thing. You know, Aurora Borealis's spell. I think Ginger may have gotten sent, um, away by mistake. Aurora warned me about extra people in the bathroom when it came up the pipes. But I thought she meant *people.*"

"Ginger went into the book?" Tuesday tugged *Sir Crispin* away from her mother and quickly began to flip through the pages.

"I'm sorry about Ginger, sweetie. I really am."

"You sought to end the enchantment by casting another?" Septimus demanded. "You consulted a sorceress?"

Kally couldn't even look at him. "Well, in a manner of speaking. She calls herself a past-life explorer and psychic counselor, but I think that's kind of the same thing as a sorceress."

"And part of this witch's spell involved trapping Sir Crispin and myself in the privy chamber at exactly noon?"

Kally didn't respond. It all sounded so sordid when he put it that way.

"Mom, Tim, look!" Tuesday held the book wide open and pointed to a beautiful, two-page illustration of a red-gold fish rearing up in the middle of a lake. It spouted a whole fountain of water, balancing a thin silver sword at the top. "It's Ginger! She's in the book, Mom, and she's huge!"

"Was that there before?" Kally asked.

Tuesday shrugged. "I dunno. I don't think so. But doesn't it look just like Ginger, only about a million times bigger? See? She helps the Dark Knight get his sword. It says so."

"It does look like my sword," Septimus commented, peering at the page. "I certainly didn't get it from a fish, but if that's how the bards wish to frame the story, to make it more magical..."

"So Aurora's spell did work," Kally said dully.

"Aurora? Is this the name of the enchantress?" Cris leaped to his feet and thumped one large fist against his massive chest. Aqua-blue eyes sparkling, he roared, "Though she may be the mightiest and wiliest wizard in all Christendom, still I shall not tarry. Until the Fair Rosaminda is freed from the evil spell of the Sorceress Aurora, upon my oath, I shall not rest."

Kally stifled a sigh. Crispin really was something when he got wound up. Too bad the lights were on but nobody was home.

"Lead me to the sorceress!" thundered the Golden Knight, and he headed for the front door, waggling his sword.

"But you don't even know where she lives. Come back here! And put down that sword," Kally ordered.

Following close behind Sir Crispin, Tuesday yanked on his arm. "I know where she lives. Come on, Cris, I'll show you."

"Tuesday, you are not taking Cris down to Aurora's," Kally warned. "He'll run her through. Or at least scare the pants off her."

"Yeah, well, if he does, then she won't try to get rid of Cris and Tim again, will she?"

Tuesday scooted out the door, her hand in Sir Crispin's, as Kally and Septimus tried to follow.

"Wait." Kally put a hand to the Dark Knight's chest. "We can make better time on the fire escape. It ends practically at Aurora's door. This way."

She reversed direction, racing through the apartment and out the window, rapidly descending the black iron stairs. But there was a decent leap between the bottom step and the concrete sidewalk, and Kally hesitated. She never had been much of a jumper.

"My lady, allow me."

Septimus edged past her, dropped easily to the ground and then held out his arms.

"I can't." She knew Cris and Tuesday would be

pounding out the front door and down the steps any moment, but still she hesitated.

He smiled a rakish grin that lit up the whole street. "'Tis no different from leaping down castle walls for a bit of fun with a saucy demoiselle, with her brothers and father following hard upon."

"And do you do that often?"

"Not often enough." His smile widened. "Never lost a damsel yet."

"I'll bet you haven't." Shaking her head, Kally closed her eyes, imagined herself falling neatly and painlessly into Septimus's waiting arms. And jumped.

She felt a jarring rush of air and then the hard comfort of the Dark Knight's embrace.

"Prettily done," he whispered. "I should be cursing you for trying to send me packing without so much as a by-your-leave. Instead, my dear Kally, I find myself simply wanting to hold on." His breath was hot and ticklish next to her ear. "And what think you? Now that I have you in my arms, should I tan your pretty hide? Or mayhap I should kiss you senseless till you admit to all the world you don't want rid of me?"

She stared at him, drinking in his stormy eyes, just a hint darker than bittersweet chocolate, at the way his thick, black lashes shadowed the sharp angles of his cheekbones, the way his mouth softened the elegant tilt of his jaw. And she wished with all her might that he would kiss her again.

"Perhaps," he murmured, his voice low and silky, "you will realize that a devoted, ardent knight is not such a terrible thing to behold."

He held her fast. His lips moved nearer. She closed her eyes.

"Kally? What the hell are you doing?"

The irate voice, coming from only a few feet away, brought everything to a screeching halt.

"Are you actually groping some weirdo on the street? You?"

Kally scrambled out of Septimus's embrace. And almost tripped over her ex-husband.

"Brad," she gasped.

"Brad?" Septimus echoed in a very dangerous tone. "The small weasel of an ex-husband?"

"Please don't start anything—"

"Weasel?" Brad echoed. His face suffused with color under his thinning blond hair. "What's that supposed to mean?"

Kally covered her face with both hands. Life as she knew it was going down the tubes.

And then it got worse.

"Daddy!" Tuesday called, waving at him from the stairs. Sir Crispin brought up the rear, his sword in his hand.

Kally tried desperately to think of some explanation she could give Brad, something to cover two strange men who'd been staying at her place, Crispin's odd clothes, the sword, the embrace with Septimus... It was hopeless.

Maybe she could just melt into the sidewalk.

"Hey, Daddy, what are you doing here?" Tuesday asked, running the last few steps and giving him a hug.

He hugged her, but above her head, he narrowed his

pale blue eyes at Kally. "I was worried about you," he declared. "And now I'm even more worried."

"But I'm fine, see?" She twirled in front of him, arms outstretched.

"Oh, yeah. Fine. You're running around by yourself while your mother is slobbering all over this long-haired Chippendale dancer."

"What is a Chippendale?" Septimus growled in her ear. "Should I run the weasel through?"

"No," she told him. "Not now."

"Mommy, were you and Septimus slobbering? Isn't that what babies do? Why would you and Tim do that?"

"We weren't." She glared at Brad, who should've known better than to say ugly things in front of his daughter. "Daddy is just being rude. And acting like a bad example."

But Brad wasn't giving up. "Let me guess, Kally. You had Big Blondie baby-sitting so you and the dark one could make out on the sidewalk?"

Septimus took a step forward. "Methinks the weasel is besmirching your virtue."

"Baby-sit?" Crispin roared, brandishing his sword. "Methinks he casts aspersions on my manhood."

Kally wondered what would happen if she just collapsed in a heap right there. Would the overpowering tide of testosterone ebb a bit? Or would anyone even notice?

She chose to try to make peace. "Septimus, Crispin," she said, in a calming voice, with a hand on each one's chest to hold him back, "this is Brad, my ex-husband, Tuesday's father. Brad, these are my friends visiting from Wales. They're not strippers or dancers of any kind. They're knights. You know, like the ones at Medieval Land. And right now they think you're insulting them, so they're getting testy. It would help everyone if you would all calm down."

They regarded each other warily, grumbling under their breath, but backed off a little anyway.

Even though they'd been divorced for years, Kally still knew Brad very well. He had ego to spare, and he hated it when he was around anyone who cast him in a shadow. The knights were not only better looking than he was, but they were also about twice his size. In terms of appearance alone, they were surely driving him crazy. Plus there was no way anyone else was going to get a share of the spotlight when Crispin was there in all his golden glory, tightly wrapped in peacock spandex and toting a five-foot gold sword.

She could see Brad bristling. The big baby.

"I don't know if I can allow Tuesday to stay here," he said in a snotty tone. "Around all this chaos."

"It wasn't chaos till you got here," she lied.

"Then why is that guy running around in a leotard carrying a sword? And why was the other one hauling you around like a sack of potatoes?"

Kally stopped in mid-thought. She had no answers to any of it. For once in his life, Brad was on the money. That was a scary thought.

Besides, it was pretty rich of him to accuse *her* of living a chaotic life. That was the big reason she divorced him, after all—because his job was unstable, he was never around, and he was totally unreliable. She grew up, past the fanciful dreams of a husband who was an actor, an artist, a dreamer. But he didn't. Even once it was clear he was never going to make it as an actor.

Once she had a child to think of, Kally was no longer willing to live Brad's crazy, shaky, fly-by-night life.

Except now *she* was the one with the crazy life. And to have it turned around on her was really, really annoying.

"Oh, right," she said finally. "Like your life is a well-oiled machine."

He pressed his lips together in a thin line. "I don't wave swords around in front of my kid."

"You do so!" Kally retorted.

"Daddy, you even showed me how to die like Hamlet, remember?"

He grumbled something under his breath and then retorted, "Well, okay, but at least I'm not screwing around in front of my kid."

"How dare you? I'm not, either!"

"Both of the he-men are staying with you, aren't they?"

"Like you haven't had half of Manhattan's out-of-work actress corps staying at your place one time or another."

"That's different."

"Mommy, Daddy, please don't fight." To her mother, Tuesday whispered, "Mommy, I think you better say something to Tim, because he looks really cranky."

She glanced behind her, and her heart froze in her chest. She was used to bickering with Brad. Sure, it left her frustrated and annoyed. But it obviously had a different effect on Septimus.

Right now, he looked icy, controlled, furious. His lip curled as his gaze swept Brad contemptuously. "You have sullied the honor of your lady," he said in a dangerous tone. "Upon my oath, she is *my* lady now. Under *my* protection."

Kally gulped. "I am?"

"Oh, she is, is she?" Brad shifted his weight from foot to foot, as if he were a boxer. "So you *are* sleeping together?"

"Brad, not in front of Tuesday," Kally warned, sticking her hands over her daughter's ears like she should have from the beginning. What with slobbering and making out and screwing around and sleeping together, Tuesday was getting a real education on the sidewalk. "Can we please take this inside?"

The Dark Knight edged in front of her. "I shall not tolerate your insults, knave. You shall taste the blade of my sword."

"Oh, yeah? Well, you haven't got one, big boy," Brad snarled. "And it looks like your pal who *has* got a sword has other fish to fry."

Even as they spoke, Cris apparently decided he'd had enough of standing on the sidelines. Or maybe he'd glanced at the stairs to Aurora Borealis's place and remembered why he'd set out from the apartment in the first place. At any rate, he suddenly took off down the stairs to the den of the psychic counselor brandishing his weapon, bellowing, "Sorceress Aurora! Your spells do not deceive me!"

That gave even Brad pause. "Uh, Kally, I think Big

Blondie's train has jumped the track, if you catch my drift."

"Nobody cares," Kally said stiffly, "about your drift." She took Septimus's hand in hers and tugged on it until he bent to listen. "You can fight with Brad later. But if we don't stop Crispin now, he's going to slice and dice poor Aurora, and we'll all be in big trouble."

"I care little for your enchantress," Septimus returned, still glaring at Brad. "If she is indeed the source of this infernal enchantment, mayhaps the Golden Nincompoop can sort it out."

"Do you really think the Golden Nincompoop can sort anything out?"

"No," he admitted, grudgingly taking a step away from his conflict with Brad. "But this is far from finished. Mark my words on that, weasel."

"They're marked, Samson."

"It's Septimus," Tuesday corrected.

As they backed up, Kally ordered, "Tuesday, stay right there by Daddy until Septimus and I get Cris away from the door."

"Mommy, I want to come, too," Tuesday cried, running down the stairs after them. "I want Ginger back."

"Huh?" Brad looked confused. "Who's Ginger?"

"My goldfish," Tuesday explained patiently. "She got taken when the spell came up the pipes."

Aurora finally opened her door, and her yelp of fear when she saw Sir Crispin and his mighty sword drowned out whatever else anyone was saying.

"By all that is holy, I command you to end the evil enchantment now!" he thundered.

Kally grabbed one arm and yanked him with all her might, while Septimus took the other one. They couldn't quite pry the huge knight out of the doorway, but he wasn't getting any farther in, either. And the pressure Septimus was putting on his wrist pretty much immobilized the sword, which was reassuring.

"Uh-oh." Aurora's face paled under that mop of orange hair, and she dropped back a step, which only made Cris try harder to lunge forward. "So I take it the spell didn't work."

"It did so work," Tuesday said smartly, squeezing in around the grown-ups to face Aurora. "Only you took my goldfish, Ginger, by mistake, and I want her back. And I want you to promise to not cast any more spells to try to send the knights away, because they're staying, and that's that."

"Well, it's not my fault about the goldfish. I told your mother there was no guarantee. And I wouldn't cast another spell for any of you if my life depended on it," she said loudly. "I'm out of the spells biz. Got that?"

"Okay, well, if I'm not getting Ginger back, I guess the rest of that's good enough for me," Tuesday agreed.

"End your enchantment on the Fair Rosaminda," Sir Crispin ordered her. "Free her from her imprisonment now."

The man was built like a tree trunk. Even with both Kally and Septimus pulling on him with all their might, they weren't getting anywhere.

"I don't know anything about any Rosaminda," Aurora snapped. She tried to push the door shut, edging Tuesday out but only stubbing Crispin's toe. "If she's in prison, I can't help her. Tell her to get a lawyer like everybody else."

"Come on, Cris," Tuesday told him. "She's not going to do any more spells. Let go."

But he growled low in his throat, brushing the little girl aside like a fly. Kally shouted, "You don't touch my kid, mister!" Without thinking, she dropped her hold on his arm and gave him a good swift kick in the left calf. Meanwhile, her pint-sized dynamo of a daughter planted herself and took a big bite out of his right kneecap.

Yowling, he dropped his sword, hopped on one foot and then the other, and finally lost his balance, toppling over like a giant redwood in a lumber camp. He lay there on the ground, holding his knee and moaning.

With his entire mass clear of the door, Aurora slammed it shut with a final clatter. They could hear the bolt slide across.

Septimus stood back, his eyes tracing a rather stunned path between mother and daughter. "I feel sure I could have protected you without—"

"Honey, you're not supposed to bite," Kally said weakly.

"Who are these people?" Brad demanded. He had backed up to where a small knot of passersby stood cheering on the combatants. "I thought it was bad enough you were involved with two strippers. But this is even worse. Even weirder. Spells and voodoo and fistfights on the street. What were you thinking?''

Kally was mortified at the public display they were putting on. Luckily, a cab screeched to a halt half a block away, laying on the horn as it narrowly missed a parked car, sparking a new uproar that the crowd hurried to catch.

She took her chance to make a clean getaway. Head down, she hurried to the apartment building lobby with her daughter, her ex-husband and the Dark Knight trailing behind. Crispin was still groaning on the basement stairs, but Septimus had the presence of mind to pick up his sword.

''Kally?'' Brad tried again. ''Are you going to give me any reason I shouldn't pack up my daughter and get her out of this insanity right now?''

Because you don't have custody or the right to take her without it? Instead, she said calmly, ''We'll talk about it when we get upstairs.''

As they reached the second floor landing, Tuesday ventured, ''Mommy? I'm not going to live with Daddy, am I? Just because I bit Cris? I'm sorry I bit Cris. Really.''

''It has nothing to do with that,'' she said quickly. ''Don't worry, baby. We'll figure it out.''

But she was dizzy with dread. What was she going to tell Brad to make this go away?

As if her problems weren't already bad enough, she heard a moan coming from the stairwell. ''Rosaminda...''

The Golden Baboon was following them. Just what they needed.

Brad waited till they hit the fifth floor before he launched another salvo. "Kally, I've been thinking about it, and there is no way my child is going to live with you in this occult ménage à...whatever."

He was lucky she didn't kick him like she had Sir Crispin. "It wasn't occult. It was just a misunderstanding. A culture clash or something." She lifted her chin. "As for the other part, I'm not even going to dignify that with an answer."

"Mommy, what was that that Daddy said, about a mirage or something?"

"Something bad that I'm not telling you about," Kally said sternly. She opened the door, pulling her daughter close and nudging her inside. "Something Daddy never should have said."

If Tuesday did not know what a ménage à trois was, it appeared Septimus did. And he didn't take the reference kindly.

He clenched his jaw into a murderous line and said fiercely, "You dishonor your lady as well as myself. You will regret your words when my sword meets your spindly neck."

"I can take you." Her ex-husband bristled.

Septimus slapped the big gold sword into Brad's hands. "You may use the Golden Dunderhead's blade. My own lies inside."

"Okay by me," Brad answered. "We can do this on the roof. I practiced up there for my stage combat class. Plenty of room, and nobody to interfere."

Kally's head began to spin. How many crises could she avert? How many times could she pull her life from the edge of the abyss?

In the thick of his macho battle with the Dark Knight, Brad bragged, "If you think you're getting a pushover here, forget it. I'm no civilian. I played Laertes for a hundred and fifty performances, you know. And I trained with Mel Gibson's stunt double's understudy from *Braveheart.* Yeah, that's right. *The* Mel Gibson."

"Look, I hate to point this out," she said, turning on him, "but Mel Gibson is an actor. What he does is pretend. With rubber swords and fake blood. And when you were Laertes, you lost every night, remember? Hamlet won, and you ended up dead."

"Everybody ends up dead in *Hamlet.*"

"Okay, well, let me put it a different way. You know stage fighting. Septimus and Crispin know the real thing."

"Oh, yeah?" Brad's vanity had been bruised again, and he wasn't giving in. "Well, I was so real in *Peter Pan* they had to give Captain Hook stitches after the matinee."

"Because you fell on him!"

"You'll see," he blustered.

"Never fear, m'lady," Septimus said with a certain sardonic edge. "I shall not slay your weasel. I'll simply teach him a lesson."

"That's comforting."

Okay, so he was defending her honor, and she appreciated the sentiment. But she wasn't exactly happy with him, either.

"People here and now do not duel on the roof, Septimus. It isn't done." She added, "You can get arrested."

"M'lady, you can keep us in the hall forever, but it will not sway us from our purpose." Septimus had a gleam in his eye she'd never seen before. Still, she recognized the fire of a man with a mission, a man who knew what he had to do and was going to see it done come hell or high water or one small female in the way. "I am sworn to uphold your honor. And uphold it I shall."

"You can't—"

But he sidestepped her neatly, letting himself into the apartment in search of his sword.

"You can't do this!" she called after him. "I will not allow it."

Meanwhile, Brad stayed out in the hall testing the sword, lunging and poking the walls with it.

"Stop that," she snapped.

He didn't, of course.

Absentmindedly, he glanced at her. "Tell him I went ahead to the roof to get the feel of the terrain, okay?"

"No, I won't tell him," she muttered, but she knew it wasn't going to make any difference. The door to the roof said Roof on it in foot-high orange letters, and she already knew Septimus could read. He'd gone through every magazine in the apartment plus Tuesday's encyclopedias all the way through *R*.

She pushed the door open, ready to try again to convince him to give up this insanity, just as the man came striding out with his silver sword. He gave her a devilish smile, and she knew there was no way she was going to talk him out of it. Men. He was enjoying this chance to prove himself.

At least she could stop Tuesday from following. "Oh, no! They may be willing to act like kindergartners, but you're not going to watch."

"Mommy, I've seen Daddy fight with swords lots of times. I even practiced with him on the roof before."

"Not this time."

But she hadn't counted on Crispin, who finally wandered up to the fifth floor. "Who stole my weapon?" he demanded.

"Um, my daddy has it."

Crispin's face reddened. "Wherefore did the brigand pilfer my blade?"

"Up on the roof," Tuesday supplied, leading the way before her mother could catch her and impress upon her that wherefore meant why, not where, and she shouldn't be helping these ridiculous men with their ridiculous sword fight!

She scrambled to catch up, racing up the stairs to the roof, intending to catch Tuesday and get her to safety.

But when she swung open the door, she saw Septimus outlined against a blue, blue sky, the sun glinting off his shiny silver blade, his long, gorgeous dark hair blowing free in the soft summer breeze. Her breath caught in her throat.

He turned, his eyes captured hers, and he bowed, tipping his head slightly. "My lady," he whispered. "I am yours."

Oh, my. Something deep inside her shifted, moved. Something quite primeval. *He was hers. And she wanted it to be that way.*

Any other currents on that roof vanished into the summer sky. It was as if the two of them were all alone.

Until Crispin bellowed loud enough to stop an elephant in its tracks. "Down below!" he cried. "It is the Fair Rosaminda!"

"Hey, I see her, too." Joining him at the street side of the rooftop, Tuesday waved her arm above her head. "Oh, pooh. She didn't see me. She got on."

She pointed to a long, rather dingy bus at the curb five stories below, where a small line of passengers trickled through the front door while people disembarked from the back.

Kally didn't much care what Rosie did with the mass transit system, but Sir Crispin certainly did. As the bus belched black smoke, he shouted, "I must save the Fair Rosaminda from the fire-breathing monster!"

Surveying the roof wildly, he grabbed his sword out of Brad's hand and leaped over the side of the building.

Chapter Eleven

They raced to the edge and saw Cris, sword in hand, attempting to climb down the side of the building.

Kally gasped and clamped her hands over her eyes, envisioning him splattered on the sidewalk. But when she peeked, she could see he was doing quite well, using a pipe and the brick facing for handholds until he got to the fire escape. From there, it should have been easy. But he didn't seem to realize he'd hit stairs and was using his mighty arms to carry him down the outside of the fire escape.

"Cris, you can walk!" Tuesday shouted helpfully. But her words blew away in the breeze. "Mom, is he going to be okay like that?"

"I don't know." She chewed her thumbnail anxiously. Much as she recognized Crispin was a nuisance, she also didn't want to see him go splat on the concrete. "Septimus, isn't there anything you can do?"

"I am called upon once again to pull the Golden Dunderhead out of harm's way?" He set his jaw. "I suppose I have no choice. If my lady asks it, then I must oblige."

"Not the—" she began, but Septimus was obviously bright enough to take the stairs and not try to climb down a five-story building.

People were starting to gather below, pointing and gesturing at the human fly descending so resolutely down the building.

"Hey, buddy, jump! Jump!" some nut screamed.

"He's not going to jump. He's that what's-his-name, the spider guy!" someone else yelled.

A news crew arrived, and cameras were pointed at the big peacock with the sword. How did they get there so fast? Kally stepped back from the edge, unwilling to get her face on the news. She had side-stepped the last public humiliation and landed right in the middle of another one. Besides, she was supposed to be home sick from work. She just knew it would be her luck to be on TV when her boss tuned in for the evening news.

"Oh, no. The police," she whispered, as the wail of a siren neared. What next?

"What is all this racket?" someone demanded behind her in a very cranky tone.

Mrs. Krasselbine.

"Well, if it isn't noisy Miss 5B. I should've known you'd be involved. Don't you know it's a violation of your lease to be up on the roof?" Clomping her cane with every footfall, the old woman was positively glowing with triumph. "I've got you dead to rights this time, missy. This is the end of the line. All I have to do is tell my son, and you'll be entertaining your Gypsies and sword swallowers on the street like you deserve!"

Sword swallowers? Kally ignored that one. "But this has nothing to do with me. It isn't what it looks like. I swear!"

"Are you or are you not on the roof? That's enough right there to evict you."

Brad advanced on Kally from the other side, clearly unhappy to have been left without a fight or even a weapon. "Looks like you're dating a real winner, Kal. You notice he ran off before we even got started. But you can tell him for me that this isn't over." He screwed up his face in an expression he'd probably stolen from a Clint Eastwood movie. "You tell him I'm not through with him yet."

She'd had about enough of this. Poking a finger into his chest, she said savagely, "You should be down on your knees thanking your lucky stars you got off this easily, you dope! Septimus is, well, he's really good at that sword-fighting stuff. He's a pro! He could skewer you and cook you over a campfire before you even got your stupid sword out of the holster!"

Brad fell back, his mouth hanging open. Kally realized, belatedly, that she'd never, ever talked to him like that. She'd never *really* lost her temper. Oh, she got irritated fairly often. Even insulting. But all-out, blazing, hot-as-a-firecracker mad, never. Not till now.

She blinked. It felt kind of good, actually.

Until Brad found his tongue and opened up, all wounded and whiny, and Mrs. Krasselbine tried to comfort him and upbraid Kally at the same time. Caught between them, Kally did her best to tune them both out.

Tuesday stayed out of it, too, thank goodness. Kally

had enough of her wits about her not to want to fight in front of her daughter. She told herself she'd been severely provoked and it wouldn't happen again.

Besides, Tuesday was more interested in what was going on at street level than the silly adults up here with their silly squabbles. So was Kally, for that matter. But she couldn't get over there to see, not with one ex-husband and a vicious old lady blocking the way.

Kally leaned to the side to wave her arm at Tuesday, who was still standing sentry. "What's happening, Tues? Everything all right?"

"Cris got all the way down okay," Tuesday relayed happily.

Kally called out, "But what's he going to do when he gets there? Rosie's bus has to be long gone by now."

"Nope. The bus is stuck. There's a police car that parked itself across the whole end of the street. Now nobody can get out," her daughter noted, gesturing wildly and jumping up and down with pent-up energy.

"Don't hop around. You could fall over, you know."

"Aw, Mom. There's a brick wall here. I'm not going to fall. Hey, everybody's really mad down there. Do you hear the honking?"

As a matter of fact, she did. Well, if the bus was blocked, maybe Crispin could board it and drag Rosie off, ending this crazy charade.

"Hey, Mom, Cris is almost to the bus." Tuesday sent her mother a cheeky smile. "Do you think he'll get Rosie to come out? It's kind of romantic, isn't it?'' She glanced down. ''Uh-oh.''

''What uh-oh?'' What could happen now? ''Is it Septimus?''

Quickly, Kally pushed her way out of the wrangle with Mrs. Krasselbine and Brad. When she was beside her daughter at the edge of the roof, she followed the path of Tuesday's gaze. Yes, Septimus had joined the melee, but he wasn't the uh-oh part. He was trying to ford through a sea of news crews and onlookers to get to Cris.

But the enraged, impassioned Golden Knight had already shoved his way past them, intent on the bus he thought had swallowed his beloved. He struck at its back bumper with his sword, but that didn't even dent its New-York-traffic-tested hide. Seeing an opening when the police car backed up a few feet, the bus began to move. It rumbled a few feet from Crispin as he swung his sword above his head.

Pretty dangerous stuff in that crowd. Kally held her breath.

A mounted policeman tried to get at Cris from behind, but the Golden Knight reared back and knocked the cop clean off the horse.

''He hit the policeman, and he's stealing the horse, Mommy,'' Tuesday reported, wide-eyed. ''That's bad, isn't it? He's gonna be in big trouble now.''

''We all are,'' Kally whispered, holding her daughter close.

The two of them watched, shocked and dismayed, but engrossed despite themselves, as Cris galloped after the bus.

He slowed, matching the lumbering pace of the vehicle, handling his steed perfectly, his golden locks flowing behind him as he saluted its side windows with his sword. But the bus couldn't squeeze past the clogged traffic, and it stopped dead, forcing Cris to steady his horse alongside it. And then he tried to slash at an open window!

People were screaming, running away from the horse, scrambling to get away from Sir Crispin and his mighty weapon. Even the policemen backed off. The police in the car seemed unsure whether to move out of or into the path of the bus, and their car jerked back and forth a few times, siren wailing.

Everyone was shouting and honking, and the bus driver must have hit the accelerator, because a big plume of noxious fumes erupted out of the back. Kally could smell bus exhaust all the way up on the roof.

"Mommy, Cris stuck his sword in the bus!"

"Ouch." Not only had he lanced the poor bus in the side, but his blade had gotten stuck below the belt of a men's underwear ad, giving it a rather risqué tilt.

A few reckless passengers forced the door open and fled the bus as Cris stood up on his horse like a trick rider at the rodeo. It was actually quite impressive. Everybody seemed to stand still, pausing to admire the spectacle of the tall, heavily muscled knight leaping off his horse right onto the roof of the smoke-belching monster.

There was a collective oooh, even a few cheers.

"They think it's cool," Kally stammered. "The guy is insane and they'rc cheering."

Unfortunately, the bus driver chose that moment to

lurch forward, knocking Crispin to his knees, dislodging the sword from the underwear ad, and dumping a middle-aged lady out the door and onto the street. The unmanned horse whinnied wildly, rearing.

Kally gripped the brick rail at the edge of the roof, craning her neck for a better look, holding her breath in apprehension. This was getting scary. Too scary. People were going to get run over or trampled if someone didn't do something.

So someone did.

Out of nowhere, Septimus emerged from the crowd in a blur of dark hair and clothes. Quietly, with a minimum of fuss, he swept up the woman who'd fallen, neatly depositing her on the curb and out of harm's way, and then the sword, which he tucked through his belt. Next he grabbed the runaway horse's reins, managing to soothe it into submission with what appeared to be a combination of sweet words and gentle strokes.

"Wow," Tuesday whispered, and Kally knew just how she felt. Now *that* was a hero.

After maneuvering pedestrians away, he bounded up the steps into the bus. "Why is he doing that?" Kally asked, but she got her answer when he exited a moment later, pulling a reluctant Rosie behind him.

"He's boosting Rosie onto the horse, Mommy," Tuesday said doubtfully, her small, troubled face swinging between the scene below and her mother. "Is he going to ride away with Rosie?"

"I don't think so. I—I don't think he would do that."

She hoped. All she needed was for the Dark Knight to ride away into the sunset with the Fair Rosaminda, leaving her to stew on her rooftop and the Golden Knight to throw a hissy fit back on the street.

Crispin had stumbled to his feet looking a little punch-drunk but still raring for a fight. Septimus whistled, waving his arm, motioning toward the horse, and Cris apparently got the message. With another mighty leap, he sprang from the bus onto the back of the horse, mounting behind Rosie. Sir Crispin grinned, playing to the crowd, lifting his arm in triumph.

He reached down and grabbed his sword from Septimus, which made Kally groan. All they needed was for the big lug to get into more trouble waving that thing around.

Even from the roof, they could see the news crews cranking, shooting more and more footage of the Golden Goon cradling his ladylove on the back of that horse. They probably thought it was romantic that he'd climbed down a building and lanced a bus, all for love. It didn't hurt that Cris, with his flowing golden locks, looked like the very picture of a hero, even if he wasn't one.

"Septimus was the one who saved the day," Kally muttered.

As Crispin milked the attention, the crowd cheered wildly, Kally shook her head with disbelief, and Septimus disappeared into the crowd.

Slowly, people began to disperse—even the policemen backed off, which really surprised Kally, since she was sure Cris would be arrested for something.

She caught a glimpse of Septimus by the police car, and she was seized with the sudden fear that maybe *he* was going to end up the fall guy. "I'd better get down there," she told Tuesday. "You stay here with Daddy, okay?"

But her daughter, her ex-husband and Mrs. Krasselbine insisted on trailing behind her, all talking at once, as Kally raced down the stairs to the lobby. It only got worse when she hit the street, where someone stuck a microphone in her face and demanded, "Do you know Sir Lancelot?"

"Don't know anything," she mumbled, shielding her face from the cameras.

"He's Sir Crispin," Tuesday said helpfully. "Sir Lancelot wasn't in this book."

"So you *do* know the big guy with the sword, huh?" asked the reporter, a pretty redhead Kally recognized from the evening news. The woman motioned for her cameraman to focus on Tuesday as she scribbled in a skinny little notebook. "What's his real name? Where he's from? Why he was all bent out of shape at that bus? Oh, and what's your name, hon? Is he your dad or your uncle or something?" She paused, her pen poised.

"I..." Tuesday looked to her mother for guidance.

"She doesn't know him. She doesn't know anything. She just thinks he looks like someone in one of her books." Head down, Kally grabbed her daughter and edged around the persistent news hound.

"I knew I shouldn't trust a kid." Thwarted, the redhead turned her attention to Brad and Mrs. Krasselbine, who were one step behind. "Either of you know anything?"

"Bradley Kevin Malone," he said with a big smile,

giving the camera his good side. "I'm an actor, and I—"

Another reporter, this one a short man with a loud tie, jumped in. "An actor? On this picture?"

"What picture?" Brad asked.

"This picture. The Mel Gibson movie they were shooting on this street today."

"Here? Today?" If Brad's mouth hung open any farther, it would hit his knees. "Excuse me." And he went scooting off in search of anyone with any hiring power.

"You mean this was all part of a movie?" The pretty reporter muttered an oath under her breath. "That blows my whole story angle."

"Didn't you hear that?" newsman number two jeered. "They say Gibson forgot to get the right permits or something. But the other one, the longhaired guy, straightened it out with the cops."

"Long *dark* hair?" Kally inquired.

"Yeah." The man shot her an impatient look. "Black hair, black T-shirt. He's around somewhere. He's the one who got the cops to cooperate. Too bad. I was hoping they might bring out the SWAT team, blast the guy off the back of the bus. Now that would've been a story."

The one who got the cops to cooperate. Septimus. But how could he have done that? He lifted a hand, and suddenly horses, policemen, ladies who fell down in the street, even reporters were sorted out and handled. Was there nothing Septimus could not do?

She raised a shaky hand to her head. And how did

a knight fresh off the Round Table come up with a cover story involving celebrity movie stars?

"So if this is a Mel Gibson movie, where's Mel Gibson?" demanded the redhead from TV.

Kally backed away fast before anyone connected her to Crispin and starting asking questions. She'd only gone a step or two when she came up hard, right against Septimus.

She knew it was him without even turning around.

"You shouldn't be here," he murmured in her ear. "Nor the princess." He hoisted Tuesday into his arms, balancing her against one shoulder, out of reach of the noisy crowd.

The image of her daughter held so securely in his powerful embrace was enough to melt Kally's heart. "I was worried," she told him quickly. She took his elbow and leaned in close, making sure her words didn't carry any farther than his ear. "I saw you with the policemen and I was afraid somehow *you'd* get carted away."

He frowned. "'Tis still dicey whether the Golden Goat can escape with his hide. I would leave him to his fate, but I fear he'll implicate you and Tuesday in his misfortune."

Exactly what she was worried about. Still, it was nice to know that Septimus was safe. Even if the hard length of him, snuggled so close, didn't feel safe in the least. All in one piece, however. Definitely all in one piece.

But right now she had other things to worry about, more important than how warm and smooth his skin felt under her fingers. "Do you know where Cris is?"

she whispered. "Is there any chance we can grab him and get out of here?"

He managed a grim smile. "None. I believe he is engaged in what these people are calling a 'photo opportunity.' On the horse, with the girl, lots of teeth and muscles."

"This is pathetic," she said with some spirit. "You're the one who did everything. And where did you get that story about Mel Gibson?"

He shrugged, but she could see the spark of humor deep in his dark eyes. "Your weasel mentioned him. Don't you recall? Brad boasted that he had learned to wield a sword from some underling of the great thespian Gibson, whoever that is. Since he expected everyone to be impressed, I thought perhaps the sheriff's men would be, as well. As for the stratagem that a movie was being filmed, I could think of nothing to explain the Golden Dunderhead's foolishness except that it was scripted. I have seen the like on your television box."

"It was very clever of you," she told him. Even in this maelstrom of activity and chaos, she found a smile for him. And the one she got back seemed very warm and intimate. Tipping her head to one side, edging in a little closer, she decided she was starting to be really glad he'd popped out of that book. "You know, I—"

But she never got to finish that thought.

"Excuse me," a very irate voice interrupted.

"Not you again." Reluctantly, she let go of Septimus's arm, turning to contend with Brad.

"If you have a second, Kally," her ex said with a snide edge. "I know there's no movie here and never was. Would you like me to start talking to a few reporters and let them know that these madmen are your houseguests?''

''Daddy!'' Tuesday cried. ''Why would you do that?''

Brad didn't answer. He glared at the Dark Knight and snapped, ''Oh, yeah, and let go of my daughter while you're at it.''

''I think perhaps we should take this upstairs,'' Septimus said coolly, casting a dark eye at the milling reporters. He wheeled, still toting Tuesday, and led the way into the apartment building.

Kally caught up to him at the first landing. ''When you said upstairs, you didn't mean the roof again, did you? I mean, you and Brad aren't going to go back to the sword thing?'' She was breathless from rushing to intercept him, and her words came out in a tumble. ''I would really appreciate it if you would just cool it on that score, because I really don't think it's good for a seven-year-old to see people fighting with deadly weapons in front of her.''

''Aw, Mommy!''

Kally went on, ignoring the objection. ''And besides, those news crews could probably see you from the street, and they'll connect the swords to Crispin.''

''I have no intention of engaging your weasel in combat. My apologies, m'lady. You are right, as always.''

''Good,'' she said with relief. She was a little surprised he'd given in so easily, but she wasn't going to quibble. ''Let's not even go near the roof, okay? Because Mrs. Krasselbine doesn't need any more excuses to get us evicted." She stopped. "Whatever happened to her, anyway?"

"The crone?" he inquired. "I dealt with her."

Kally paled. He'd offered to slice her into little pieces the first time. "How?"

"I related the same rather pallid story about the movie star, and how honored she must feel to live in a building soon to be famous. I suggested that the great Gibson person might want to meet her." He shrugged. "It seems she's happy to oblige most anything from a handsome face."

"Whose? Yours or Mel Gibson's?"

This time he couldn't keep back a self-satisfied grin. "I believe in using every weapon in my arsenal."

"I'll just bet you do."

"Uh, if you two are through, could we get a move on?" Brad asked peevishly.

They'd delayed long enough. After scaling all five flights of stairs one more time, Kally let them all into the apartment, steeling herself for another battle. But it never materialized.

First, Tuesday ran off to get her Knights of the Round Table place mats to show her dad, and Brad followed, muttering something about getting his child away from all this craziness.

As soon as the others were out of earshot, the Dark Knight pulled Kally aside.

"M'lady, I am wondering if it might be best to allow the princess to accompany her father this evening. Perhaps that might smooth a few..." He lifted an eyebrow Brad's direction, but Kally felt sure she was the only one who caught the insolent gesture. "A few ruffled feathers."

"It *would* get her away from all of this."

"Just in case any of the reporters return," he added. "Or if Sir Rash-and-Reckless—whom you will recall is still mucking about down there—should happen to divulge his most recent place of residence and the reporters come calling."

"I hadn't even thought of that," Kally said slowly.

"I think your weasel also made dire imprecations concerning stealing the princess away from you, did he not?" Septimus probed. "Perhaps if she is safely under his care for a little while, his ire will cool."

"Right again." Kally chewed her lip. "Taking her home with him would probably stroke his ego, plus I'm sure a few hours of Blazer the Dragon is all it would take to convince him he doesn't really want full-time, forever custody."

"The man is a scoundrel," Septimus grumbled. "How could he not want such a fine child?"

She smiled. "Thank you," she said softly. "It really means a lot to me that you like Tuesday so much. She is a great kid, isn't she?"

"She is, indeed."

It was another of those off-kilter, warm-and-fuzzy moments she was so unaccustomed to, when she could forget where Septimus came from and just enjoy where he was now.

She let herself get tangled in his deep, bittersweet-chocolate gaze, allowing herself to wonder for the first time what it would be like to have a man like this around all the time, through long afternoons and lazy mornings, placid breakfasts and scheduled dinners. What would it be like if she and Septimus were regular old folks with normal, boring lives?

It would be heaven, a small voice inside her whispered.

But a new spate of honking and sirens from outside her apartment broke her reverie, reminding her that nothing about her situation was normal.

"I think you're right, Septimus. About tonight and Tuesday. *If* she wants to go. I won't make her." She called, "Tuesday? Could you come out here a minute, please?"

Her little girl came bounding on the run. "I was showing Daddy my princess outfit." She paused, twisting her mouth to one side and tugging at the hem of her yellow T-shirt.

"Is something wrong?" Kally asked.

"Mommy, I think I should go to Daddy's house tonight." She dropped her voice, whispering behind her small hand. "Don't worry. I'll talk to him about Tim and tell him Tim is A-okay and that it wasn't all a big mess here like he thinks. Nothing about the book, though, and how they got here." The child pretended to zip her lip. "That's our secret, right, Mom?"

"Good idea."

"And if he wants to know about Cris, I'll just say that Cris is so in love with Rosie it made him kind of nuts, so he made up the stuff about the enchantment." She grinned. "Like on 'Melrose Place.' They always fall in love and go nuts."

Kally shook her head. She was really going to have to put the kibosh on Tuesday's new fondness for adult soap operas. "Let's get your toothbrush and pack some things. If you're sure you want to go to Daddy's."

Tuesday nodded firmly. She was acting like a spy ready to go behind enemy lines for the good of the resistance, and Kally didn't like it at all. But for the very first time, she knew in her heart her daughter's life would be calmer and more normal if she were staying with her father.

How had her life come to this? She had always been the one on the even keel, the sensible one, the one with the reins of her life firmly in control.

Well, not anymore.

"Mommy, I'm ready to go," Tuesday called, and Kally gave her a hug and a kiss, warned Brad he had better be responsible and stressed to both of them that this was just for tonight. Although there was still a certain testiness in his eyes when he looked at Septimus, Brad acceded, scooping up his daughter and her paraphernalia and finally leaving Kally alone.

Alone with the Dark Knight.

Kally hadn't thought this through that far. All alone with Septimus. She swallowed, wondering what to do next.

"Do you want to—?" She knew what she wanted, and it was a pretty scary idea. So she took a different, less dangerous tack.

She started again. "Should we be thinking of another trip down to the street to see what happened to Crispin?" she asked reluctantly.

To pick up Cris's trail, she was probably going to have to go down all those flights of stairs. But she was already exhausted from running up and down so many times. What she really wanted to do was mix a batch of margaritas and curl up on the sofa and watch *My Fair Lady* a few times, till she forgot all about her troubles.

"He's a battle-tested knight of the realm who has survived many adventures. 'Tis certain sure he will emerge from this escapade unscathed." He scowled. "I am well acquainted with Sir Crispin's ability to arise smelling like a rose, no matter what swamp he falls into."

"I suppose." Kally dropped onto the couch, too tired to stand any longer, and switched on the television out of habit. "But what if he tells people he came out of a book? And leads them here to prove it?"

Quietly, Septimus slid beside her on the sofa. "If he is to spill his secrets, I fear we cannot stop him," he said softly. "And he may already have done so. Even *he* is unlikely to have tarried, posing for pictures, this long."

Idly, Kally let her head drop to his shoulder. It felt so comforting, so right, to be lounging here with the Dark Knight. "I think it's awful, how they were making such a fuss over him," she said. "You were the real hero, Septimus, and Tuesday and I know that, even if no one else does."

"Ah, but you two are the only ones who matter to me. Who cares what accolades are showered upon the Golden Goat?"

She snuggled closer. How long had it been since she had someone to ponder her troubles with? Okay, so if she was being fair, those troubles were partly because of him. But it wasn't Septimus's fault that he'd gotten nabbed out of a book and thrown into twentieth-century New York. And he really was awfully helpful and sweet. And warm and strong...

She let her eyes drift shut. Beside her, Septimus settled her into his lap, adjusting their positions to make her more comfortable. Keeping her eyes closed, she smiled. Now *this* was normal. And very nice.

His lips drifted to her ear, and then the side of her neck, grazing, teasing more than kissing. It felt wonderful. With another man, she might have been worried about things spinning out of control. But not Septimus. After all, he'd taken all those vows of honor and virtue and whatnot. Surely he was safe for a few soft kisses and a little cuddle. No harm there.

Kally relaxed into the sinful, delicious feel of Septimus's warm lips, slipping her fingers into his thick, sleek hair, lifting her mouth to his....

On the television, a sharp female voice announced, "There was an amazing turn of events on the Upper West Side today, when an apparently lovesick man carrying a sword climbed down a five-story building to impress his girlfriend."

Kally sat up fast. It was the redhead from earlier in the afternoon.

"Oh, no. It's on TV. All of it," she whispered.

The screen dissolved to footage of Sir Crispin, resplendent in his bright purple leotard, manfully descending the side of the building. They cut to him on the back of the horse, cuddling Rosie to his massive chest and smiling broadly.

"After stealing a mounted policeman's horse and

impaling the bus the young woman was on, this man, who apparently calls himself the Golden Knight, vanished into the wilds of Manhattan with the girl and the horse.'' The reporter pasted on a small, knowing smile. ''Another unidentified man tried to convince police it was all a stunt from a movie, but that turned out to be pure fiction. Police are looking for this Golden Knight character, as well as the other man, for questioning. So you might want to be on the lookout for a big gorgeous blond guy with a very long, uh, sword. He's a keeper.''

Snicker, snicker.

''He disappeared into the wilds of Manhattan? They're looking for him—and you—for questioning? Oh, my God. We're going to have to do something about this.'' Kally choked.

''But not right now.'' Septimus reached for the remote and switched off the TV with one click. And then he pushed her down into the soft cushions, pressing his body into hers from stem to spine-tingling stern, finding her mouth, branding her with a hot, deep, sinful kiss that shocked her to her socks. ''We have better things to think about,'' he murmured, and the insinuating pressure of his body made his intentions clear.

In her mouth, on her skin, deep inside, she felt alive, warm, moist, sizzling. But her mind went completely numb.

Wow. Her self-control was shaky, but she found enough left to pull away a few inches. ''I—I didn't think you—we—could do that,'' she managed to say.

"What about your code of honor? Aren't you sworn to uphold virtue and all that?"

Septimus gave her a dark smile. "I think you've mistaken me for a different knight, my lady. I'm the wicked one, remember?"

Chapter Twelve

"You don't mean that." She blinked. "Do you?"

"Yes. As a matter of fact, I do." He held back for a second, bracing himself on his elbows, his dark eyes full of heat and desire as he gazed at her.

"W-wicked?" she echoed. Why did it sound so good?

"As wicked as you like." He leaned closer to nibble her earlobe, biting on the pink tip, making her shiver with pleasure. "At a time like this, the last thing I want to think about is virtue."

"Me, either." She slid her hands through his thick, lustrous hair, raising herself and tugging him down to meet her mouth. It had been so long since a man had held her, she felt like she was shooting off sparks wherever he touched.

"Sweet Kallista," he murmured, twisting enough to bring her beside him, sliding his hands along the curve of her bottom, clasping her so very near.

The sparks had escalated into a bonfire. His T-shirt was soft under her hands, his shoulders wide and strong, and her fingers began to tingle. She felt a sense of anticipation, of magical, momentous events just about to happen.

But his long, lean body was hard next to hers, insistent, tantalizing, *real.*

Real. Why did she have to think of that?

"Septimus, wait."

"What is it?" She saw the dark light in his eyes, the caution banking his hunger.

"I... I don't think I can do this," she whispered.

After a pause, he drew back. Darkly, he inquired, "Should I venture to ask why, m'lady?"

Would it be too utterly ridiculous to say *Because I'm not that kind of girl?* "Because..." She couldn't look him in the eye and stick to her principles. So she cheated and lay back on the couch, staring at the ceiling. "Because none of this is real. It's a total fantasy."

"Is this real?" he asked, fiercely covering her mouth with his, blazing his kiss deep into her soul. His arms tightened around her, holding her close enough to feel the heat rising from his body, to sense the rapid, erratic beat of his heart. "Is this a fantasy?"

She was breathless, dizzy. She licked her lips. "I—I can't pretend I don't want you, Septimus. That would be a lie." Her voice grew huskier as she allowed herself to feel him, close and hot and overpowering. "I want you so much even *I* can't believe it."

A heady silence loomed between them. Finally, he lifted one dark eyebrow. "And?" he asked. "You want me, but..."

"But I don't know," she cried, scrambling away to sit up. She pulled up her knees and covered her face with her hands. "I'm very confused. Very tired and mixed up and chicken."

"Chicken?"

"Cowardly," she explained. "I'm a coward. I like my life to be neat and orderly, without this kind of surprise. I don't—" She hazarded a glance his way. "I don't want to tingle! I don't want to make an emotional investment in you if you're just going to be gone tomorrow."

"Where would I go?" he asked dubiously.

"That's even worse! So you're only here because you don't have anywhere better to go?"

"Kally, 'tis you I want." His words were soft and reassuring, and he stroked her cheek ever so tenderly, brushing aside the wispy tendrils of her hair. "'Tis with you I want to be."

"I wish I could believe you." Again, her gaze flickered over him. Did he have any idea how drop-dead gorgeous he was? "Septimus, I'm the only woman you've even met here. How do you know it's me you want?"

"You do both of us a disservice," he said dryly. "I have met several women who tried to catch my eye, including your friend Rosie, the more mature lady who fell off the bus, and a young damsel at the clothier who seemed rather intent on acquiring my phone number, whatever that is. And while my memories of my former time, my former place have begun to fade, I remember clearly a variety of ladies, pretty and plain, sweet and waspish. Still, Kally, you are the only one who has so enchanted me."

"You hardly know me. I hardly know *you*," she

replied. She knew she was letting panic seep into her words, but she couldn't hold it back. This had been a really horrific few days. "And what I do know, well, it's not like it's the kind of thing you hear every day. 'So, Kally, who are you dating?'" she mimicked. "'Oh, the Seventh Son of the Lord of the Lake of Midnight. Great guy.' 'What does he do for a living?' 'He's a knight of the Round Table. And how's *your* love life?'" Miserable, she covered her face with her hands. "See what I mean?"

"I see," he said softly, "that my timing is terrible."

He tipped her to one side, tugging the cushions out from under her, and then swept her into his arms long enough to set her on a chair.

"What are you doing?" she demanded.

He winked at her as he came back with a load of bed linens. "Making up your bed."

"But—"

He put a finger to her lips. "It seems very clear to me, my dear lady Kallista, that you have exhausted yourself trying to find ways to carry the burdens in your life. What with disarming me and telling lies to protect us and cooking for the Great Golden Appetite, sharing Tuesday's narrow little bed, racing onto the roof and down to the street four or five times, consorting with sorceresses, fending off the weasel and the crone... It's no wonder you are not receptive to my advances."

Not receptive? If she'd been any more receptive they'd be rolling on the floor naked by now. She spared a moment's regret that they weren't. "Are you really making my bed?"

"Yes, I am." He tossed the pillow on after the sheets. "I fear I am not as tidy as you are, but it should suffice."

It looked incredibly inviting. Kally slid into the bed with a good deal of gratitude, still wearing her jeans and T-shirt. "Where are you sleeping?"

"With you."

Quickly, she scooted off the bed. "No way that will work."

"I am too long for Tuesday's bed," he explained. "And so are you. I have had enough of the floor, m'lady. I suggest we both behave ourselves and share this one, in the interests of a good night's sleep."

He seemed perfectly serious. But he was the one who'd said he was the wicked knight, the one who didn't care about virtue. "Can I trust you?" she asked doubtfully.

"Upon my honor." And he lay his hand over his heart.

One night sharing the same bed couldn't hurt, could it? Kally climbed in and rolled to the very edge, closing her eyes, willing herself to sleep. She was so very tired, after all.

As she lay there, he slid onto the bed next to her and stretched out his long legs above the sheets, not touching her anywhere. And then he clicked on the television. He really was turning into a pretty standard-model twentieth-century male, what with watching TV all the time.

Kally smiled into her pillow when she recognized what he'd chosen to see. It was a video. A video she knew very well, down to the last note of the "Breathing Fire is Fun" song. Blazer the Dragon.

She snuggled into the bedclothes. He might not be real, but he was one heck of a guy.

"MOMMY? Are you awake?"

Kally opened one eye. "Tuesday? Is it morning?" she mumbled.

Groggy and confused, she tried to decide if it was day or night, if she was supposed to be at work and why it felt as if someone were breathing on the back of her neck. Someone very warm and very heavy, if the arm and leg slung around her were any indication.

Breathing? Arm and leg? Oh, no.

"Septimus!" She shot up, knocking him away. At least he was fully clothed. Thank God for small favors. She vaguely remembered drifting off to sleep on opposite sides of the bed, him above the covers, but sometime during the night they must've wandered a little closer.

Breathing. Arm and leg. A *lot* closer.

Kally took a deep breath. Nothing had happened. They were both dressed. Not one thing had happened. She searched her memory just to be sure. Okay, so she had slept quite deeply and had some very vivid dreams.

Kally felt her face flush with hot color.

Shoving a handful of hair away from his eyes, Septimus sent her a hazy smile, taking in the whole blush. "Good morning."

"Good morning." She smiled. She couldn't help it. He looked all soft and cozy, and her stomach felt fluttery just looking at him. Before she could stop the thought, she wished once again that things were different. Wouldn't it be nice to wake up to that every day?

"Mommy?" her daughter interrupted. "Why are you guys both in the same bed?"

Kally closed her eyes and took a deep breath. "Well, sweet pea," she said quickly, scooting off the mattress and looking for her shoes. "We just fell asleep here. I don't want you to think anything happened, like, you know, on 'Melrose Place.'"

Tuesday shrugged and jumped onto the bed with a big thump. "Okay."

Kally ran her hands through her hair, hoping that would wake her up and clear her head. "What are you doing home so early, anyway?" Her heart dropped into her toes. "Where's your dad? He didn't come up with you, did he?"

"Uh-uh. Daddy has a job in Central Park today. I wish I coulda gone with him, but he has to juggle fire or something, and he said no."

"Juggle fire? Where is he working?" she asked, straightening her clothes, trying hard not to glance at Septimus.

"A fair or something. Incense Fair?"

"Renaissance Faire. That's lords and ladies and knights. Like Septimus. You know, he might enjoy that." She gave him a quizzical stare.

"I might indeed," he replied, offering a crooked smile. "Perhaps the three of us could make a day of it?"

Feeling very happy all of a sudden for reasons she

couldn't quite figure out, Kally leaned over and gave her daughter a kiss on the top of the head. Must be the benefit of a good night's sleep. "It might be fun if the three of us went to the fair. Would you like that, Tues?"

"Way cool, Mommy." Tuesday vaulted over her favorite knight and landed on the floor. "So who was watching the Blazer video? It's still in the VCR."

Kally inclined her head toward Septimus. "He fell asleep watching it, I think."

"I like the little dragon." He pounced on Tuesday, making her squeal when he tossed her over his shoulder. He sang, "Fire breathing is such fun. You know, it doesn't happen to just anyone…"

Kally smiled. *The three of us,* she thought again. *This feels really right.*

Tuesday ran to toss her little suitcase on her bed while Septimus hit the shower, but Kally basked a moment in the warm, sunny feeling of being part of a family. It took her breath away.

She didn't have long to savor the good mood before Tuesday came racing back, carrying the familiar robin's-egg blue book.

"Mommy!" she cried, her eyes wide, "the book is changing!"

Relieved that was all it was, Kally busied herself folding the bed away. "I already knew that, hon. Or at least I thought so. I mean, Septimus's name suddenly appeared, and then his part seemed to get bigger. Oh, and Ginger showed up, remember?"

"I know, but now, Mommy, it's really different! Look."

Tuesday held up the book, displaying the cover front and center. The swirling gilded letters were gone, replaced by thinner, more elegant silver ones.

Sir Crispin, the Golden Knight of Yore had become *Sir Septimus, the Silver Knight of Yore.*

Kally stared. Hastily, she snatched the book and riffled the pages. Every single word had changed. Now it was all about Septimus. She scanned the first page, about how he was born the seventh son of the Lord of the Lake of Midnight and ran away from that cold, unhappy castle at a young age to make his way in the world. Even though she was stunned, she was also sentimental. "Look, it's Septimus when he was little. Isn't he cute?"

"Mom," Tuesday protested. "Keep going. Wait till you see what happened to Cris."

"Okay, okay." She flipped ahead, looking for a mention of Sir Crispin. But she stopped about halfway through, when the Silver Knight was invited to a feast at the palace of King Alardyce, where he was to meet his betrothed, the Fair Rosaminda. "Her again," she groaned. She peered at the illustration. "You know, she does resemble Rosie. That is really annoying."

"Mom," Tuesday said again. "Go on. You haven't gotten to the good part yet."

"Okay, okay." She read on, finally finding Sir Crispin, but he was a bit of a buffoon in this version, a minor nuisance character. "Justice at last," Kally said with a laugh. "But wait, he's running off with the Fair Rosaminda. And Sir Septimus says she's a faithless strumpet and he doesn't want her anymore and rides away into the forest, where he finds a damsel...." She swallowed. "Imprisoned in a tower?"

Kally dropped the book, her voice a small, rusty squeak. "Oh, my God. He's climbing into the tower to save the beautiful Lady *Kallista.*"

"Yeah, Mommy, isn't it awesome? Except for she has long hair, she looks just like you!"

"No, she doesn't." But shc rctrieved the book and intently studied the pictures and the words. The woman was so pretty, so spunky, so brave, battling an evil sorceress and a dwarf, jumping off the tower wall into the arms of her beloved Silver Knight.

How could that be her? She was a coward, a wimp, afraid to fall in love, afraid to lose her heart, afraid of everything.

"I think it's kind of stinky *I'm* not in there," Tuesday grumbled. "I mean, if you and Tim are in the story, don't you think I should be, too?"

"Maybe you come later," Kally whispered, still in shock. What did this mean? That she would end up with Septimus in real life? Just because a book said so?

And why did the very idea scare the pants off her? And give her a major thrill at the same time?

She had gotten no farther than the page where the Silver Knight knelt in front of Lady Kallista, asking for her hand, when the doorbell rang. "Honey, will you get that?" she asked absently.

"It's not a person, Mom. It's a piece of paper."

"Oh, okay. Bring it over, will you?"

"Um, Mommy?" Tuesday hesitated. "I don't think you're going to like this."

She looked up. "Why not?" But she recognized the stationery before she read the words, and her heart sank. KAR, it said in big, ugly letters. Krasselbine Apartment Rentals.

She began to read aloud.

> "You are hereby notified that complaint(s) have been lodged against you by your neighbors, specifically Ms. Aurora Borealis in #1B and Mrs. Edith Krasselbine in #4B. The boxes checked below indicate the nature of the complaint(s). As per your lease, section 14, paragraph d, you may be subject to eviction and/or damages for these violations pending determination of the validity of said charges."

There were big check marks next to "excessive noise," "loud/unruly visitors" and "harassing or frightening behavior." The "other" category was also marked, with "illegal use of roof" written in a quavery hand that could only be Mrs. Krasselbine's.

The really sad thing was that she couldn't fight any of the charges. They were all true.

Septimus entered, still wet from the shower, rubbing his hair with a towel. "So, where is it we're off to? We shall have a day of merriment and..." His voice faded when he saw their faces. "Something has happened. What is it?"

"We're getting evicted," Kally said flatly. She handed him the letter.

"Well, you shall no longer be imprisoned in *this* tower, at any rate," he said wryly, as he read it over.

"You don't know how tough it is to find towers in this town," Kally told him.

As she spoke, the phone rang, and she moved to answer it, fully expecting it to be the KAR office, notifying her exactly when she had to be out. Instead, it was a voice she knew—the voice of her supervisor from the Department of Immigration and Naturalization.

So just how bad was this going to be?

"Mr. Johnson," she said quickly, verifying how late she was with a glance at the clock. She should have been there an hour ago, if she was going in, which she wasn't. "I'm still home sick," she added. "The flu or something. Barfing all night. I would've called already, of course, but I've been, uh, sick."

"Kally, this isn't like you," he said in a grumpy tone. "You're never sick. And we have people lined up all the way down the hall, and nobody knows where your files are."

She sagged against the couch with relief. At least he wasn't calling to report he'd caught a glimpse of her on television during the Golden Knight's antics.

"Look," Mr. Johnson went on, "if you're really sick, why then, you're entitled to rest and get better like anyone else. But you'd better be sicker than you sound, Kally. I don't go for goldbrickers or malingerers, you know."

No, she didn't know. In fact, she'd never heard those words before in her life, although she guessed they meant people who pretended to be sick when they weren't.

"I'm really sick, Mr. Johnson. And I do have lots of sick days piled up, since I never, ever use them."

"I suppose." Abruptly, he said, "Gotta get back to work here. This place is insane this morning."

"I know what you mean," she whispered, as her supervisor rang off.

"Apartment, job... What next?" she asked, wondering if she could convince Aurora Borealis to send them all into the book. Okay, so there were ogres and swamps and evil wizards. At least she wouldn't be getting evicted and fired right and left.

"Um, Mommy," Tuesday called from the direction of the TV. "You better come and look at this."

"Don't tell me—"

"The Golden Dunderhead," Septimus finished for her.

"I was going to put in my Blazer video again, but before I could, that reporter lady, the one who was asking us all those questions yesterday, she broke in to 'Regis and Kathie Lee' for a special report." Tentatively, Tuesday added, "She said Sir Crispin was spotted swimming in the East River."

"The East River?" Kally hurried in front of the set. "Why would he do that?"

"Lindy Dale here, live," the flashy redhead droned, "not far from Gracie Mansion, where earlier I attended a christening ceremony for a new fountain."

She waited, and eventually, the screen filled with an image of the mayor smashing a bottle of champagne against the side of a rather clunky fountain.

"Some moments after that, the mayor invited a group of VIPs, this reporter among them, to ride out on the city's new yacht, the *SS Big Apple,* to inspect the entire East River Drive promenade from the river. But as we did so, the man reporters are calling the Golden Knight was spotted, attempting to swim after us.'' She paused, adopting a more sorrowful tone. ''I have a personal angle on this story, friends. I last saw the Golden Knight, or Sir Crispin, as he invited me to call him, at about seven—''

''What? Why would she be with Cris at seven in the morning?'' Kally broke in. ''He's hardly the type to get up early to meet a reporter for breakfast.''

The look on Septimus's face stopped her cold.

''No way. You think Crispin...'' She lowered her voice significantly. ''You think he spent the night with the redhead? What about Rosie?''

He shrugged. ''Methinks our Golden Popinjay prefers the damsel with access to cameras and lights.''

''And she was going for an exclusive?''

He arched a cynical eyebrow. ''Something like that.''

Well, Ms. Lindy Dale *had* seemed awfully interested in Cris's muscles and, uh, sword. Kally shook her head. If she was nuts enough to want the Golden Goon, so be it.

''What's she saying now, Tues?'' Kally asked, trying to get up to speed on what she'd missed.

''Something about how Cris is enameled of her—''

''Enamored?''

''Uh-huh,'' Tuesday continued. ''And she didn't know he followed her to the river, but when she went off on the boat, he must've come after it thinking she was in danger.'' She raised wide eyes to her mother. ''She says he thought a tugboat was a sea monster.''

''Yes, that's right, friends,'' the reporter finished with a flourish. Her tone had elevated to pure theatrics. ''Although reports that this man, this Sir Crispin, is an escaped mental patient are unconfirmed, it does appear his grasp on reality is shaky enough that he looks at a common tugboat and instead sees—'' she licked her beautiful crimson lips ''—a sea monster.''

Kally let out a long sigh. Cris was headed for Bellevue as sure as shooting.

''He also claimed to be a recent immigrant from a town in Wales called Glinn, although no reference to this town has been found on our maps at KBAC, and sources at Immigration and Naturalization are unable to confirm any of these details.'' She tipped her head to the side, still looking sad but composed, as fake as a paint-by-number Mona Lisa. ''Although we do not yet know whether this demented man has survived his plunge into the East River, police and rescue crews are working steadily. They are asking anyone with any information about the mysterious Sir Crispin to please call the hot line number now flashing on your screen. And remember, if he does survive,'' she intoned dramatically, ''he should be considered armed and dangerous.''

''This is insane,'' Kally muttered. ''This Lindy person is making this up as she goes along.''

''Should we call the hot line, Mommy?''

''No, I don't think so.'' Against her better judgment, she took Tuesday's hand. ''I think we'd better go down there. Whether we like it or not, we let him loose on the city, and we're responsible."

Septimus nodded. "And if he has indeed drowned, someone should be there to mourn him."

"You don't think he's drownded, do you?" Tuesday gasped.

"Sir Crispin?" Kally shook her head. "Not a chance."

"He does have a certain ability to defy the odds," the Dark Knight noted sardonically.

"I also think that Lindy Dale knows more than she's telling. All that stuff about not knowing whether he was alive or dead. If she was watching him, she has to know." Kally grabbed a scarf and some sunglasses to wear as a makeshift disguise. "Here, Septimus, squash your hair as much as you can and put on this baseball cap. We don't want anyone picking you up for questioning on the bus-impaling thing."

"What are we going to do with Cris if we find him?" Tuesday wanted to know as she danced ahead of the others.

"If he is still alive and kicking, somebody has to get to him and tell him to keep his mouth shut," Kally said with feeling. "And maybe even convince him to stop making such an ass of himself."

"Best of luck, m'lady. Best of luck."

The Dark Knight's eyes were alight with mischief, and Kally didn't know whether she wanted to kiss him or hit him.

Or maybe both.

Chapter Thirteen

As they made their way to the park near the mayor's mansion, Kally tied the scarf around her head and jammed on the dark sunglasses. At least it was a sunny day, so she shouldn't stand out as too suspicious.

It seemed silly braiding Septimus's hair so they could stick it up under a baseball cap, but Tuesday absolutely loved it. She was enjoying it so much, her mother had to remind her he wasn't a doll she could play hairdresser with just for fun. He didn't fuss at all but let the little girl fool with his gorgeous hair all she wanted.

And once it was done, with his hat and a pair of dark glasses, he looked pretty good. But then, he looked pretty good no matter what he did.

They could hear the sirens and the whirring of helicopter blades overhead even before they got there. There were police everywhere, on horseback and motorcycles, even a few boats lined up, but Kally kept her little party well within the clumps of curiosity seekers, happy to find camouflage.

There was no sign of Crispin, which was just as well. If he showed one hair of that golden head, the fleet of cops would descend and scoop him up before anyone had a chance to shout, "Keep your mouth shut!"

In fact, the only evidence that he'd been there were a few disintegrating pieces of armor and a very corroded slender sword someone had pulled from the muck. The East River had apparently melted his once mighty blade into a nail file.

"Okay, the sword I understand. But armor? He wasn't wearing his armor when he left, was he?" Kally asked.

"Whose else could it be? There aren't any other guys with armor and swords around here, Mommy. It has to be Cris."

"Yes, but..." He might have had the breastplate on when he climbed down the building, but that was definitely it. The rest of his stuff should have been in a pile in the corner by her kitchen. Now that she thought about it, she couldn't remember seeing it there the last time she looked. "He came back and stole it! He must've!"

"Is that of import?" Septimus inquired. "If he did return to your lodgings, he did not stay. And we still do not know where's he's run off to now."

Meanwhile, Tuesday spotted Lindy Dale, girl reporter, near the fountain from her broadcast, and they angled over that way. As soon as she was off the air, they intended to see what they could find out. But they were intercepted before they got anywhere near her.

"Kally, Tuesday!" someone called loudly, and all three of them stopped dead in their tracks. So much for disguises. They wheeled, ready to face the music.

"Phew," Kally muttered under her breath. Just Rosie.

"Did you see Cris on the news?" Rosie chattered. Although her face was a little flushed, she seemed to be in her usual good humor. "I was on the stationary bicycle at work, riding along, and this thing about Cris came on the overhead TV. I couldn't believe it!"

"We were a little shocked, too," Kally replied. "We thought he was with you."

"Yeah, right." Rosie stacked her hands on her hips, and her expression was decidedly peeved. "He dumped me last night to go after that witch reporter, Mindy or Cindy or whatever. He decided she was his little rosebud instead of me, and he left me with that stupid horse. I took it to the police station, of course. But, man, I could've got in such trouble."

Kally patted her on the shoulder. "Oh, dear. I am sorry."

"Yeah, me, too. I think he could've gone somewhere if we could've kept him on the weights," Rosie said dreamily. "Just a little body sculpting and some technique, and man, he could've taken Mr. America." She shrugged. "But he was getting bummed with the work, even in just one night. He saw that Mindy girl talking about him on TV while he was doing the stair stepper, and he took off, just like that. I really miss him, though. Best-looking guy I ever dated."

"Rosie, was he wearing armor when he left on the horse with you?" Kally ventured. She was still confused on that score, and she didn't see why she shouldn't quiz Rosie a little.

"Uh, no." Rosie pressed her pretty lips together, but it was obvious there was more she wasn't saying.

"Come on, spill it," Kally ordered, taking her neighbor's arm and leading her aside.

"You're going to be mad at me," she whined.

"Try me."

"Well, he's really goofy about that armor. He, like, loves it or something." Rosic shook her blond curls with exasperation. "So while you were downstairs and he was posing for pictures on the horse, he made me go upstairs and get it. It was really heavy, too. I stuck it in a Hefty bag and stashed it for him. It was just a favor, since him and me were, like, running away together."

Kally was getting really tired of this starry-eyed stuff. "But you only ran as far as your health club."

"Yeah, I know. But it seemed romantic at the time," Rosie said awkwardly.

"Rosie, here's some advice. Stay away from Cris. He's in a lot of trouble. And stay out of my apartment, too, will you?"

Noting the sharper tone, Septimus grabbed her from behind before she got into a fight, which was a good thing, really, since Rosie was in a lot better shape than she was.

"The comely Lindy has concluded her report," he murmured in her ear. "Time to make our move."

"So you think she's comely, huh?" Kally gave her the once-over. "I think she's a little hard."

"Fine. The hard Lindy has finished her report. Are you ready?"

As he pulled her along, Kally filled him in on what

she'd learned from her neighbor. "Rosie broke into my apartment while we were gone, do you believe it? I'm not sorry to be evicted from that place, what with one neighbor who thinks she's a spy, another one who's conjuring up spirits in the basement, and a third one who's a burglar."

"And when I said you were imprisoned in a tower, you doubted me," he said mockingly.

"Don't push me," she replied.

"Me?"

But she didn't have time to spar with Septimus just then, no matter how much fun it was. Lindy Dale was refreshing her lipstick and frowning into a mirror, and they had to catch her before she went on the air.

"Lindy? Can I speak to you for a moment?" Kally asked politely.

"Do you have a tip or something?" She turned, dismissing Kally and her odd headscarf with a single glance. "Nah. Guess not."

But then her gaze tripped over Tuesday. The child stood behind her mother.

"Hang on. You're the kid I talked to yesterday. You told me his name was Crispin, didn't you? And guess what? It is." Narrowing her eyes, Lindy knelt at Tuesday's level. "So, hon, do you know something, after all?"

"We're more interested in what *you* know," Kally interrupted, shielding her daughter with her body. "We saw you on television trying to pretend you didn't know whether he was alive or dead, but I think it's all a scam. You saw him, didn't you?"

"All right, keep your voice down, will you?" The

redhead chewed her perfect lip gloss and glanced around to make sure no one was looking. Her voice a whisper, she admitted, "So I saw him get out of the river. Big deal. He was dirty and wet, but otherwise okay. I even managed to talk to him. I told him he was stark raving bonkers and he better get a move on or he'd get carted off to the nuthouse for sure."

"So if you knew he was okay, why did you put on the big manhunt, with the search boats and all the police and everything?" Kally demanded.

"Are you kidding?" Lindy Dale laughed shortly. "It's a much better story this way."

"Okay, so where do you think he went?"

"No clue." She turned to go. "Although he was totally wacked over losing his stupid armor. Big surprise—everybody knows you could melt a tank in the East River. Maybe he said something about replacing his armor. I don't know." She wandered to the fountain, signaling to the cameraman that she was ready to go.

Kally mused, "Replacing his armor? But where?"

Septimus inquired, "I don't suppose armorers hang about in shops here?"

"Uh, no. But they do hang around—" Kally grinned at her daughter "—at the Renaissance Faire. Which is where we were all going, anyway."

THE RENAISSANCE FAIRE was being held, aptly enough, within sight of a castle. The turrets and towers of Belvedere Castle overlooked a Shakespeare garden, as well as the outdoor theater where Brad would have loved to play Oberon or Benedick at the New York

Shakespeare Festival. To the north, the great lawn stretched out, where famous singers serenaded big concert crowds, where Disney had been known to premiere a movie or two.

Bright-colored tents and pennants ruled the day. Women in low-cut bodices and full skirts and petticoats waltzed by, carrying baskets of cakes and posies to sell, while vendors hawked all manner of food and drink. Actors dressed as royalty were far grander, all velvet and silk, with elaborate hats and funny pointed shoes. There was even a jousting field at one end.

Tuesday wanted one of everything, of course, from the flower garlands for her hair to the pointed cone hats and the jingling jester caps. Crystals, candles, jewelry, pewter dishes, miniature swords, tankards, chess sets, crockery and pots—this was like Wonderland for a child who loved the world of chivalry. Wide-eyed, the child rushed from one booth to the next, with the words, ''Can I have it, Mommy?'' permanently affixed to her lips.

Kally remembered why she'd kept Tuesday away from the Renaissance Faire.

Still, with effort she could hold back her daughter's buying spree. Which only left the search for Crispin and a niggling sense of anxiety about Septimus to worry about. After all, this was almost like sticking him back in his old world. He'd handled the culture shock of a one-way voyage just fine. But how would he react to a round trip?

Septimus gazed around with perfect calm.

''What do you think?'' she asked cautiously.

''Interesting. Rather clean. And I have noted no cutpurses or whores.'' He winked at her. ''But otherwise, quite a decent replication.''

''Mommy, what's a—''

''Never mind.''

''Oh, I know what *that* is,'' Tuesday protested. ''But what's a cutpurse?''

''You can ask Septimus later,'' she said dryly, holding Tuesday close so she wouldn't get lost in the crowd. ''For right now, let's see if we can find Cris, shall we?''

They visited every armorer they could find, and there were several. They poked into the tents where the chain mail fashioners hung out, and there were more of them than plate armorers. Septimus was very critical of all of their work, suggesting that armoring standards had fallen seriously since the last fair he'd attended.

In any event, no one remembered seeing anyone as large and blond and vainglorious as Sir Crispin. Except there was this one small armorer's assistant who remembered someone a little different.

''I think I saw a dirty, kind of smelly guy in purple tights. Smelled like maybe he'd just come out of a Dumpster or something. Of course, he didn't look that out of place here.'' The assistant shrugged. ''Lots of tights, you know. But the reason I remember him was I thought he might be thinking of stealing a nice piece of plate. A stainless steel breastplate. I shooed him away, though. And that was it.''

It didn't sound like the Crispin they knew. But he had been through a dip in the river. And he'd lost his precious armor. Maybe he'd lost a little of that pompous, puffed-up edge along with it.

"If it was him, we've already missed him," Kally concluded. "And it looks like he doesn't have the money to buy new armor here, anyway."

"Or the weapons to steal it," Septimus added.

But as they wound their way through the fair, they did run into Brad, who was entertaining at a small, rough-hewn stage. He alternated juggling fire with a man who walked a tightrope and a couple who did ten-minute versions of *Hamlet* and *Macbeth*.

Kally ducked the other way as soon as she saw him, but it was too late. Dousing his fiery clubs, he ran after the three of them. "What are you doing here?"

"Nothing," she said quickly. "Tuesday wanted to come. You know she likes anything to do with knights and lords and ladies and all that. She's loving it, aren't you, Tues?"

"This is so cool, Dad! It's the best place you ever worked. Much better than when you were the chicken outside Clucker's. Or remember when you were inside that piggy bank with a big penny taped to your head?" Tuesday was positively bursting with enthusiasm. "Well, this is much better than that!"

"Yeah, thanks." But he did seem to perk up because his daughter appreciated his new gig. "Hey, I saw that blond guy, the one who was causing so much trouble yesterday. He's not still living at your place, is he?"

"You saw him?" Kally demanded. "Where? Here?"

"No, on TV." Brad gave her a funny look.

"What's he got to do with you, anyway? I'm not trying to be a jerk, Kally, but I really am worried about Tuesday living there with someone like that hanging around."

"He's not. He's gone," she assured him. She could tell he wasn't going to let this drop, and once again, she was unwilling to fight in front of her daughter. "Tues, here's some money. Tell Septimus to get you both an ice cream or a pie or something, okay?"

"Okay!" And she bounded off, happy to oblige. Septimus sent Kally a searching glance, as if to ask whether she needed him to defend her from Brad. But when she didn't call, didn't ask, he allowed himself to be dragged away.

"Brad, really, Crispin is gone," she repeated.

"But he might come back?"

"Oh, no, I don't think so."

Brad cocked a thumb in the direction Septimus had departed. "And what about the other one?"

"Well, yes, he's staying with me, but that's more..." She felt herself blushing and she really wished she wasn't. "We're kind of involved."

"Involved?" he asked. "In front of Tuesday?"

Kally lifted her chin. "Of course not. But if we were, I mean, didn't you ever think that I might have a boyfriend again? Or a lover? Or even a husband?"

"No, I guess I never..."

"Well, you'd better start thinking about it, Brad. Because this just might be the one." She ran a hasty hand through the short wisps of her hair. "So far, I can't figure out where this is going. But it just may. Go somewhere, I mean."

She watched as Septimus approached, his free hand in Tuesday's, each of them gnawing on a huge turkey leg and laughing out loud. Septimus had discarded the baseball cap and the glasses, and he shook his head, sending his dark, rich mahogany hair rippling down his shoulders. Kally caught her breath.

The sun was shining, the sky was blue, her daughter was happy, and the man she loved—the man she thought she might really be able to love—was within her reach. Handsome and smart and thoughtful and a joy to be around, and he was within her reach.

What the hell was she waiting for?

The tingle she remembered feeling when she stood outside Kew's Curiosity Shop came dancing back with a few hundred brothers and sisters. Her heart seemed to stand still.

"Yes," she said softly, "this is definitely going somewhere."

Septimus bent to pull out a handkerchief and wipe a spot off Tuesday's chin, and Kally made up her mind fast.

"Brad, when do you get off?"

"In about half an hour, why?"

Softly, persuasively, she said, "Because your daughter is crazy about this place, and you have a golden opportunity to show it to her, to have a really great time, just the two of you."

"But I—"

She raised a hand. "Don't start with me. You have punked out on her and ditched her more times than I can remember." Starting to get fired up, Kally sailed on. "I need tonight for myself. I wasn't ready last night, but now I think I am. And I need you to take Tuesday, maybe for today and tomorrow."

"I have to work tomorrow."

"So do I. I may lose my apartment, and I can't risk my job, too," she muttered. "So she has to go to day camp tomorrow whichever of us has her overnight. Unless you want her to stay with Septimus. He could probably baby-sit."

"Lose your apartment?" Brad's voice rose. "Your job? And you want that Chippendale dancer to baby-sit?"

"He's not a Chippendale dancer. And I'm not going to lose my job, although the apartment is dicey. But I'll deal with that later." Kally shook her head to clear it. "You didn't want her with me right now, because my life is chaos, and I admit that's true. So you can have her. Not forever. But for tonight."

"I had her last night."

Kally crossed her arms and stared at him. "Do you want to be her father or don't you?"

"Well, of course—"

"Then stand up, damn it," she said, seethingly. "Yesterday you were threatening to sue for custody, and today you don't even want her for one night. So be a man for once in your life!"

"All right."

"All right? That's it?"

"I'll keep her for tonight or a couple of days if that's what you want. You're right," he added, "she should see the whole fair. And I'm just the one to show it to her. Besides, there's no way that Chippendale dancer is baby-sitting."

"Brad," she called after him, but he'd already gone to collect Tuesday.

And once again, she and Septimus were alone.

She knew what she wanted, but how did she explain it to him? *The various strands of my life are unraveling around me, and this may be my only chance to be with you?*

"You seem very pensive, m'lady," he noted, taking her hand in his as they walked through the park to the sidewalks of New York.

"Just thinking about tomorrow," she told him gloomily.

"Not a pleasant prospect, I take it?"

She shook her head. "I have to go to work unless I want to lose my job, plus I have to figure out what to do about the landlord's petition to evict us, I have to decide what, if anything, to do about the menace we call Sir Crispin *and* somehow convince Brad my life is calm and serene enough to keep my daughter."

"And tonight?" he asked.

Tonight. Kally smiled in spite of herself. "Tonight, I just don't want to think about any of it."

Septimus turned slowly, read the light her eyes and pulled her into his arms. And right there, in front of honking cabs and moms wheeling babies in buggies and messengers on bicycles, he kissed her.

Breathless and light-headed, she pulled back enough to get some air. As he tipped his forehead against the top of her head, as she felt the silky tendrils of his long, midnight hair brush her cheeks and her chin, Kally knew in her heart this was right.

"Tonight, what I'd really like to do," she said longingly, "is have a really normal evening. Nothing fancy. Just you and me, as if we were regular people."

"And what do regular people do, m'lady?"

She smiled, thinking out loud. "Oh, they might go to some old movie at a revival house, and eat Chinese takeout, and go up on the roof and dance, and maybe kiss under the stars."

"I don't know what a revival house is, and I've never heard of Chinese takeout, but somehow I have no fear you can teach me." He raised her hand to his mouth, brushing his lips across the back of it softly, slowly. And then he lifted his deep, dark gaze, lingering on her mouth before meeting her eyes. His voice was a little husky, quite sexy when he said, "I'm a very quick study."

"Yes," she breathed, "I've noticed."

"Hey, get a room," a passerby jeered, and Kally felt hot color rush to her cheeks.

"We should, uh, probably not be, you know—"

"Never fear. I understood the knave's remark." Septimus set his jaw and muttered, "If I but had my sword.

"Maybe the best thing is to go to my place." Kally backed up, drawing him along with her. "You can tell me all about the Lake of Midnight, and how you ran away from home when you were eight, and how you got to be a knight."

She knew he knew he was being cajoled, and neither one cared. But Septimus wasn't standing still, either. With a rakish smile, he caught her, sweeping her into his hard embrace as she offered mock protest.

"Septimus, stop!" Kally cried, but she wound her arms around his neck and held on, anyway.

He strode down the sidewalk toward her building, weaving through traffic right and left, carrying her along as if she were the lightest burden in the world. She held back a giggle as she took in the startled glances around them.

She had to admit, it was kind of fun having an unpredictable swashbuckler around.

"You're not going to carry me upstairs," she insisted, wiggling in his arms, trying to get him to let her go. "You'll die before we get up there. And besides," she whispered right in his ear, "I think you should save some of your strength."

That got his attention.

He dropped her so fast she almost fell. "Are you suggesting—"

"I don't know." She honestly didn't know. But she had a very good inkling.

"Unless you want to make love on the stairs, I recommend we retire to your chambers with all due speed," he murmured, kissing her quickly. "Lead on, m'lady."

Kally raced up the five flights to her apartment with Septimus hot on her heels. But as soon as they got inside, he grabbed a silver gauntlet and shin guard from the pile of armor in the corner and prepared to leave.

"What's going on?"

He straightened, holding himself proud and tall. "You asked for an evening lived like 'regular people,' and I intend to deliver."

"But—"

He put a finger over her lips. "It is my understanding that the man is the one who pays the way when he entertains his lady here."

"Yes, but—"

Septimus bent and kissed her again, leaving her breathless and unable to protest. "So I shall trade some silver for paper again. And then we shall have our evening."

"Yes, but—"

But he was gone.

After she got over her disappointment, Kally found she was overwhelmed with a strange feeling of joy and anticipation.

Hiding a small smile, she began to hum loudly, totally off-key. Was that "Someday My Prince Will Come"? Or "Some Enchanted Evening"?

She didn't care. Dancing over to the kitchen table, Tuesday's Round Table, Kally began to make a list.

While he was out scaring up paper money, she had to shower and dress, look in the paper for a movie, order the Chinese food, find those paper lanterns she bought for Tuesday's birthday party and string them up on the roof...

Oh, yeah. And figure out how to ask Septimus to make love to her.

Her smiled widened. Somehow, she didn't think that one would be too tough.

HE DIDN'T REALLY understand *My Fair Lady,* but he loved the Chinese food. Halfway through an egg roll, he moaned, "I love this world, that it holds such riches, such flavors. I must remember what this is. Heaven!''

Kally had her own version of heaven, and the rooftop with its string of paper lanterns was very, very close. She stood enfolded in his arms near the doorway, taking in the bright colors bobbing in the summer breeze against a black, starry skyline.

''Very pretty,'' Septimus murmured, nuzzling her neck.

She wasn't sure if he meant the decorations on the roof or her neck.

She knew what *she* thought. Much as she liked the paper lanterns and the view, Septimus was much better to look at. He'd surprised her by showing up, not just with money, but with a new pair of jeans, a white button-down shirt and a black jacket that made him look wonderful.

She'd been afraid that her pale green dress—a birthday present from her sister—would be too dressy when all he had was a T-shirt and jeans, but it turned out perfect. Even if Septimus was scandalized by the fact that her knees were showing under the hem of the short skirt.

''I thought you wanted to stay away from this forbidden territory,'' he said, spinning her to face him. ''The crone frightened you away.''

''I'm already getting evicted,'' she said with spirit. ''What else can she do?''

It felt odd to be careless and risky all of a sudden after she'd played it safe for so long. But she had discovered the fun in being wild, and she had no intention of going back now.

She punched the play button on the boom box she'd brought up, and the sound of a solo saxophone filled the roof. As she went into his arms, she knew Septimus didn't know how to dance, but it didn't matter. He was, as he'd noted, an exceptionally quick learner.

Clasped in his embrace, swaying to the music, Kally gazed at the stars. This was all so perfect, except for one small, niggling thing. *I wish,* she thought fervently, *I wish he were a regular guy with a résumé and a birth certificate, with a polio vaccine and a driver's license, so that loving him could be easier.*

"What are you thinking?" he asked softly.

For this one moment in time, she listened to her heart. Easy? Why should it be easy? The things that were worth something were always the hardest of all.

This was right. *He* was right.

Steeling her courage, searching his eyes, she whispered, "Septimus, will you make love to me?"

Chapter Fourteen

"No."

"No?" She stepped back, feeling as if she'd just hit the high end of the roller coaster and plummeted to earth.

"I'm not some sudden fancy, a whim on a roof at midnight." His lips curved into a narrow smile with just a trace of a dark edge. "Like someone I know, I do not make love lightly. I do not care to make this emotional investment if you will be gone tomorrow."

"Where would I go?" she asked softly, echoing his words when this conversation was reversed.

"Back to reality." He cocked an eyebrow. "Am I not a fantasy? A figment of your imagination?"

"I don't know what you are," she said honestly, "but I want you anyway."

"If this," he whispered, grazing his lips against her bare shoulder and then her cheek and the corner of her mouth, "if this is what you want, I won't deny you. But is it enough?"

"Yes." Her skin was dying to be touched, her mouth aching to be kissed, her knees weak with wanting and need. "It feels so real. How can it not be?"

Kneeling, Septimus drew her fingers into his, pressed a kiss against her hand and raised his gaze to hold her. "My bright, beautiful Lady Kallista," he began, in a low, unwavering tone, "my heart is yours. Whatever we are to be, wherever we are to be, know this day that I loved you."

There was something to be said for chivalry.

And then he rose, swung her into his arms with one smooth motion and strode down the stairs to her apartment.

One of her shoes fell off near the landing. The other made it as far as the door before it, too, dropped away.

"If you don't watch it," she said, wincing as he kicked open the door, "I could get used to being carted around all the time."

He shrugged, a half-smile playing about his lips. "I thought it might seem dashing to you."

"Oh, it does," she whispered, as he set her carefully on the sofa bed. She framed his handsome face with her hands, pulling him to her. "It does."

He quickly shed his shoes and his jacket, and she almost jerked a button off his new shirt in her hurry to push that away, too.

But he caught her impatient hands in one of his. "No rush, m'lady. I refuse to make love to you on the stairs, on the roof or in haste. We shall take our good time, you and I."

"I—I don't know if that's what I want."

"When you tangle with dark knights, they don't always ask what *you* want," he said huskily.

Kally smiled, sliding the shirt off his shoulders, baring his beautiful flesh, running her hands over his hard, sculpted frame. "You forget, Septimus, I know you too well. You say you're fierce and dangerous, but you're just a pussycat."

"Pussycat, am I?" Without warning, he moved. Swiftly, he flipped her onto her back and covered her body with his, pressing her hands at her sides, edging her long legs apart and settling between them.

"Is not a panther a pussycat?" He tilted to bite her neck gently, teasingly. "Is not a lion a pussycat?" His lips moved to her earlobe, and he flicked his tongue against it, making her suck in her breath.

His strong arms held her fast, his hard chest slid against her breasts, provocative and sinuous, and his long, thick hair fell in silky tendrils across her neck and face.

It felt wonderful, all of it. Wicked, bewitching and wonderful, all at the same time.

Raising her knee to cradle him, Kally closed her eyes, soaking him in. He smelled like midnight, hot and dark, like candlelight, a fine sheen of masculine sweat, her own shampoo and some mysterious scent of the forest deep. It was tantalizing, delicious.

Already she was eager and willing, ready to reach up and grab him, to force him to take her, now. But the Dark Knight was only getting started.

She could feel him everywhere, branding himself against her, imprinting the length and breadth of him into her senses, as his kisses trailed from the line of her cheekbone to the tip of her nose to the angle of her shoulder, down her bare arm. She was so very impatient, so very hungry for more.

Releasing her hands, he moved his to cup her

breasts through the pale green linen of her dress. She moaned, not quite believing that greedy sound came from her, but arching into his caress, tangling her arms around his neck, filling her hands with his fabulous mane of hair.

Even through her dress, her breasts peaked to meet his hands, and her nipples chafed against the heavy fabric. But his clever fingers slipped away, down to the edge of her skirt, where the fabric had bunched high on her thighs.

Septimus slid his fingers under her skirt, molding his hands to the naked curve of her bottom, sending little flickers of fire radiating everywhere through her body. "You are a naughty girl, my dear Kallista," he whispered. "I was led to believe that ladies of this place protected themselves with all sorts of undergarments. And yet you are as bare as a newborn babe."

And he slid one finger over the roundness of her buttock, around her thigh, barely brushing, teasing, testing the sensitive skin, until she was whimpering and wiggling under his touch.

"I—I wasn't sure what they did where you come from," she managed to say, barely getting the words past her dry, raspy throat. Oh, God, if he didn't stop that soon, she was sure she would expire right there. "I—I seemed to have this idea the ladies you would know didn't wear anything…under…and I didn't want to surprise you."

"Everything you do surprises me," Septimus murmured, his breath hot and soft in her ear, his fingers stoking her fire higher and higher.

Her dress pooled waist-high, leaving her at the

mercy of his skillful caresses, and she tried to elude him, to distract him. But he was merciless. He kept up his torturously slow pace, his agonizing rhythm, until she was gasping for breath and burning with need.

But just when she thought she might topple over the edge, he pulled away, leaving her panting, unsated. As if she were a rag doll, he raised her enough to strip away her dress, laying her bare completely. Pushing her into the cool sheets, he dipped his head to kiss her, tracing the line of her sweat-slick skin all the way from her collarbone to her knee with one slow hand. A lock of his hair brushed across her nipples, and she shivered with exquisite, uncontrollable sensation.

He bent to take the nipple in his mouth, to taste it with his tongue, and Kally pressed herself against the front of his jeans, burning too hot to be patient. She moaned again, unable to hold herself back. Rising, she slid her mouth over his powerful chest, licking, tasting, just enough to make him jump, too. She reached for his top button, but he batted her hands away. Brooking no objection, she reached again, rubbing a hand down his rigid length through the faded denim.

"You make a persuasive case," he said roughly.

"Please, Septimus. Now." Her whole body was on fire. Even one more minute, and she would go mad. "Please."

He peeled his jeans away. Bare as a newborn babe. Except no newborn was built like that. Even through the hazy, ragged focus of her passion, Kally smiled. It seemed they'd both come dressed for the occasion.

But still he held back, still he denied her what she most desired, what she was dying for.

She met his gaze, so dark and unreadable, and she wound a hand around his neck to urge him nearer. "I want you, Septimus, more than anything I've ever wanted. Isn't that enough?"

He lifted her slightly, he kissed her deep and hard, and he stroked inside her, ruthless and fierce. "I love you, Kally, and I know you love me, too. Before this night is through," he warned, "you will admit it."

She cried out with sheer bliss, with joy, with intense and amazing pleasure, as Septimus poured into her, drove her, relentless and rough.

She held him so tight she wondered how either of them could breathe. Her body climbed higher and higher, but still he defied her.

"You do love me," he told her. "Your body gives you away, my love."

But she barely heard the words. His hands and his thrusts were setting a pace she couldn't contain. Desperate, wild, she simply didn't have the will left to resist the truth. "I do," she whispered. "I do. I love you."

And he smiled, speeding up his rhythm just enough, toppling her into a shattering, rocketing release. After he found his reward, he held her close, stilling his uneven breathing.

Kally had never felt more exhausted, more spent. This had been a battle of wills. And the Dark Knight had won.

"No," she murmured. "We both won."

He dropped a small kiss into her hair, cradling her

against his chest. Relaxing, too tired to pretend she didn't want to, she snuggled closer, pulling his arm around her, clasping his hand.

Her last thought before she drifted to sleep was that she no longer had any doubts. If what they had just done together was a fantasy, then she was the queen of France.

There was no way Septimus and his wonderfully inventive body could be anything but real.

WHEN KALLY OPENED her eyes, she saw that he was already awake, gazing at her with an expression that was impossible to read. But when he reached for her, wrapping her close to his warm, hard body, melting her with a delicious kiss, she knew exactly what he wanted.

If only she could stay. If only she could forget about the real world for a few more hours, she could nestle next to him in the soft confines of the sofa bed. They could make love until both of them were too weak to stand.

"I can't," she whispered, slipping away. "I have to work."

"Kally..."

She shook her head. "Let's just leave it the way it is. Perfect." She smiled at him, so dark and devastating, yet so sweet and tempting. "I'll leave you a number where you can reach me at work if there's an emergency. Like if the Golden Dunderhead shows up." She groaned, wishing she hadn't thought about *him.*

She blew him one last kiss off her fingertips and

stepped back, as if over an invisible threshold. With one motion, she left behind the wanton Lady Kallista and regained Kally Malone, working woman.

It was very strange, blowing her hair dry, looking for earrings and panty hose, jumping so easily into the world of everyday work. She'd had the experience of leaving for work while the man in her life lounged in bed before—it was the story of her life with Brad—but it still felt odd, unsettling. Septimus's situation was different, of course—she could hardly pitch him into the street and tell him to look for a job when he was two rungs below an illegal alien—but it still made her feel, well, odd, as if she were the responsible adult and he was a wayward child.

Unfair as it was, she didn't like it.

But she put that unpleasant thought firmly aside and dressed like the mid-level bureaucrat she was, sweeping out past the sofa bed with brisk cheer. Septimus was not, as it happened, lounging in bed—he was up, with the bed made into a sofa. His hair was tousled, and he'd pulled his black jeans on.

He smiled. She stopped. Her mouth went dry.

It wasn't her fault. It was his chest. Since he wasn't wearing a shirt, it was right there, in full view, and she stared, remembering how it felt when her mouth slid across his ribs and his shoulders, when her fingers traced the ridges of hard muscle and sleek skin.

Who cared who kept whom? She was in love!

And she couldn't wait to get back, to explore some more of the Dark Knight.

"I'll be home as soon as I can," she promised, daring to drop a quick kiss on his lips before scooting away. At the door, she stopped and turned. "Do you have something to do today? You could always go to the Renaissance Faire if you're bored, although I'd stay out of Brad's way if I were you."

"M'lady, I have no shortage of ways to occupy my time." Septimus's eyes grew stormy. "I have much to learn. There are newspapers, magazines, television, encyclopedias... And I must understand it all if I am to stake out a place for myself in this world of yours."

"You already have a place," she reminded him. *In my heart.*

But as she scurried to the subway, as she rode the crowded car, as she marched down the hall and into her office in the steady stream of workers, even as she perused her mountain of files and scanned her appointments for the day, Kally's mind whirled with confusion.

This was real, this humdrum, this routine. So what the hell was that wild ride with Septimus last night?

"It was great," she said out loud before she caught herself. "Whatever it was, it was great."

She shook herself to snap out of it. Even if he stayed just the way he was, no strings attached, how could he be happy sitting in her apartment while she rushed off to work every day? He was a man of action, used to battling his way from dragon to princess and back again. How long would he stay idle, reading encyclopedias, before he took off to find some excitement?

By ten o'clock, however, she was too busy to worry about it. There was a good reason not to take sick days—things were a major mess when she got back.

She was trying to wade through the sea of pink

message slips from her two-day absence, trying not to get too far behind with all the people stacked up in the corridor, trying to figure out who'd done what to her files, trying desperately to remember the lies she'd told about her supposed illness so her stories to concerned co-workers would be consistent, and in general having a really rotten morning.

If the little red light on her phone flashed one more time, if one more piece of emergency e-mail popped up, she swore she'd kill someone.

At least the morning positively raced by, with all its hassles and annoyances. Time flew whether she was having fun or not, apparently.

Oddly enough, at the stroke of noon, things changed. Dramatically.

It started when Beth, whose office was next door, darted in just as the clock ticked high noon. Grinning like the Cheshire cat, she asked, "Got a minute?"

Kally really didn't have time for another interruption. But Beth had always been a real sweetheart, and she looked so thrilled and excited, Kally couldn't turn her away. "You look happy."

"Beyond happy!" Beth said joyfully. "Tom proposed." She thrust out her left hand, showing off a big, beautiful solitaire. "The good news is, we're getting married right away."

"The good news, huh?" Kally took the hint. "That sounds like there's bad news, too."

"Kind of. But I'm hoping it's good news for you." Beth leaned over the desk and announced, "Tom's got a new job. In Oregon. And we're taking it. That's why the rush on the wedding—he has to leave next week for Portland, and he says he can't live without me, so I'm going, too."

"That's wonderful," Kally responded warmly. "I'll be sorry to see you go, of course, but I know you've been crazy about him for a long time. No wonder you're thrilled."

"Exactly." She pushed a sheet of paper with her address scrawled on it across Kally's desk. "And you may be, too."

She took the paper, glancing at the address. "Thanks, Beth, but I remember where you live. Are you getting a going-away party together? I could help—"

"This isn't for a party. Listen, Kally," she said in a conspiratorial tone, "you know how much I love my apartment. Well, I'm out of here as of Friday, and I don't have anyone lined up to take it. I thought maybe you—"

"Are you kidding?" Kally jumped up from her desk. Everyone in the office knew that Beth had the best apartment in the city, a fabulous, rent-controlled, bay-windowed two-bedroom beauty in the Village. "Are you kidding? Of course I'll take it."

"Okay, well, drop by my office tomorrow and I'll bring the lease. You can move in any time after Friday." Beth smiled. "I was hoping this would work out. It's great for me to have it settled before I leave for Oregon. You're going to love this apartment!"

One cruddy apartment lost, one gorgeous apartment found.

Kally's head was still spinning with this incredible piece of luck when Mr. Johnson, her supervisor, strolled in. He didn't even bother to ask if he was interrupting, just walked right in and sat in her side chair.

She hastily crunched some papers together to tidy things up a bit. "I'm really sorry about Monday and Tuesday," she said quickly, "but I'm feeling much better now and I'm trying hard to get back on top of things."

"No problem, no problem," he reassured her. "Sorry about that call yesterday. I was just getting antsy to let you in on some news, a development that's been brewing a while. Your being gone was bad timing, that's for sure."

Cautiously, she said, "I'm afraid I don't understand. What news?"

"You're getting a promotion, my dear!" he declared, slapping her desk with one hand. "They're creating a new position to act as liaison to the Justice Department. You get complete control. You can hire a couple of support people, take a few meetings with the feds. It's a great opportunity, Kally."

But that was a *huge* step up. She barely knew what to say. "Are you serious?"

"Absolutely. And you deserve it. I recommended you myself. Congratulations!" He confided, "Of course it comes with a nice big raise, too."

"A promotion?" she stammered. "*And* a raise?"

"Absolutely." Mr. Johnson shook her hand heartily. "You might want to run up to the thirty-fourth floor. That's where your new office will be. Oh, and you'll be picking out your own furniture, of course. Everyone in management group does."

She sat there, planted at her desk for several minutes, utterly stunned. She even pinched herself.

This was spooky. The life that had been unraveling only a few hours ago was falling into order, and fast.

She wanted to share the news with Tuesday, of course, and Septimus, too. Wow! A new apartment and a new job and a new office and more money. What more could she ask? She glanced at the phone. Should she call? Septimus was at her place—her *old* place—while Tuesday was off somewhere with her father.

Kally pulled her hand back. Better take a few deep breaths first and get used to the idea.

She also wanted to let it sit for a while, just to make sure nobody changed his mind and snatched away her good fortune.

But her mind was reeling as she tried unsuccessfully to clear away a few things on her desk. "Kally," she told herself sternly, "you were gone for two days and these poor people were waiting for their green card applications and whether fabulous things are happening to you or not, you still have to do the work."

Concentrating fiercely, she shuffled papers, reviewing facts and making decisions, just like she did every day. As she arranged the pile of applicants whose green cards were being granted, she was suddenly struck with a very bizarre idea.

She whispered, "It wouldn't be that hard to stick Septimus in here with these others. I wanted him to have a résumé and a birth certificate, didn't I? Well, I can get him a green card, anyway."

She'd never strayed from the straight and narrow in

her life, and she almost looked over her shoulder to see if anyone was listening.

But why not manufacture an identity for her favorite knight? He wasn't that far off from the other immigrants whose files she monitored. People came to America every day without papers or identification. He just had a weirder background story than most. Why, she could make him a whole file, airtight, as if he had legally emigrated to the United States.

So she could help Septimus out a little before she left this job. No one would ever know. And if America got the chance to know Septimus, she felt sure they'd want to keep him.

There was another dimension to this newfound belief, too. So many unbelievable things had happened to her today, it was as if the world had a plan for her, a plan that included Septimus. Why should he have been sent to her in the first place if she wasn't supposed to help him? So what if it required forging a few documents here and there? It was all part of some cosmic scheme that was much greater than poor little Kallista Malone.

Secretly thrilled with her skulduggery, she set to work. It wasn't hard at all, really—she had all the forms and plenty of other people's documents to copy. With a little Wite-Out, a Xerox machine and some creativity, she had a pile of paperwork in no time, all of it establishing an identity for her favorite Welsh immigrant. She gave him a plausible birthdate and place, and applied for a replacement passport.

"I can give it all to him when I get home," she decided, glancing at the clock. Two hours till quitting time. She smiled mistily. "It'll be like a gift, like my way of telling him I want him to stay and be a real part of my world."

He was worried about fitting in and finding a place, wasn't he? And she was worried about him getting bored sitting around being an illegal alien. But this way, he could find something he wanted to do, starting out new and fresh in his new land. He was legit.

And she knew, once he had paperwork started with the government, no one would ever deny he was real again.

The relief she felt was amazing. But as she sat at her desk, fingering her handiwork, watching each tick of the clock, she knew she'd never make it till five.

All of this day's incredible good news was rising inside her like a helium balloon, choking her, demanding to be shared.

She reached for the phone. Her fingers shook a little as she dialed. It rang twice, three times, five times. But no one answered.

That was odd. Maybe he'd gone out for a minute. Maybe he was pawning more silver to buy her a present. Now *that* was a nice thought!

She'd just dropped the receiver into its cradle when the phone rang. She leaped on it, hoping it was him. Eagerly, she said, "Septimus?"

"No, Mommy, it's me." Tuesday's voice rose. "Something bad is happening, Mommy! You have to stop it!"

"Where are you? What's wrong?"

"Everything is a mess, Mommy, and it's all my fault!" her daughter wailed.

Tuesday was so bright and mature, it was often easy to forget she was only seven. Until she hit the panic button, like right now. "Calm down, Tues," her mother said soothingly. "Tell me what happened. Are you at home?"

"No, no, you don't understand. I'm at the fair. And Daddy and Tim are going to fight a duel!"

"A duel?" Another one? Her heart sank. She'd thought they were past that. "Are they on the roof again? Where are *you*, sweetheart?"

"I told you, Mommy, at the fair," Tuesday responded impatiently. "I *was* home. That's where we got Septimus. Daddy came up with me this morning when he took me home—"

"He was supposed to take you to day camp," Kally said angrily.

"I know, but I needed my backpack. And I wanted to bring the book, you know, *the* book, to show my friend Madison, and—"

"Okay, so Daddy took you home. What happened then?"

"Oh, Mommy, it was terrible!" Tuesday cried. "Septimus was on the couch and he wasn't wearing any shirt and your dress was on the floor and Daddy got really mad about a house of sin or something and he tried to hit Tim only Tim hit him first and Daddy told him he was taking me away and I would never see you or Tim ever again! He said he would sue you. For custody, is that right? Of me. And I would live with him and never come home! Mommy, he can't do that, can he?"

Her heart sank further. "He can try, sweetie. I don't think it would work, though."

But even if it didn't work, her domestic life had become a soap opera. A bad soap opera. She had never wanted her daughter to witness this kind of strife, ever. Damn Brad and his stupid male pride, anyway.

As Tuesday sniffed, Kally asked, "So now they're at the Renaissance Faire and they're fighting a duel?"

"A sword fight, Mommy. At the jousting pavilion. They're starting any minute." Tuesday calmed down a little. "They said if Septimus wins, then Daddy promises not to sue you for custody of me. But if Daddy wins, then Tim agrees to leave you and me forever!"

That was a stunner. "Why would he agree to that?"

Woefully, Tuesday explained. "Daddy told Tim he was wrecking our lives forever and that because of him we didn't have any place to live and probably you would lose your job, and if Tim had any honor he would leave us alone. But, Mommy, I love Tim. I don't want Tim to leave. Do you?"

"No, sweetheart, I don't." Kally grabbed her purse from under her desk. "You calm down and go to the jousting pavilion, so at least you're somewhere safe." She didn't pause to consider how ridiculous that statement was. "I'll be there as soon as I can. And don't worry, Tues. No one is going to hurt anyone, and nothing they decide will matter in the least. Septimus is not leaving us. And you're not leaving me."

As she hailed a cab and hurtled toward the park, Kally was fuming. She was almost as mad at Septimus as she was at Brad.

Of course Septimus would win. That was a foregone conclusion. But how dare Septimus give in to this stupid macho posturing and make things even worse with Brad? How dare he teach her daughter that force was the only way to handle a dispute?

And how dare he agree to the possibility of leaving her just because her stupid ex-husband said so?

She jumped out of the cab and raced unevenly in her heels across grass and rocks to get to the jousting pavilion. After only a few steps, she ditched the shoes and ran in her stocking feet. Still, she was huffing a bit by the time she got to the pavilion, which was really just a big, open, candy-striped tent with flags on the top. The pennants blew briskly in the summer breeze, and Kally swore under her breath at the idiocy of men to ruin such a nice day.

"Mommy, I'm so glad you're here!" Tuesday shouted, running up and grabbing her around the waist. "It's this way. They started a while ago."

As they rounded the tent into a long, flat, open area, Kally saw that the two men had already worked up a sweat, their heavy silver swords crashing through the air, as a gaggle of onlookers cheered for one or the other.

No matter who they were cheering for, Septimus clearly had the upper hand.

She caught her breath. He really was good at this. And he sure did look fine while he did it.

Cleanly, with a minimum of fuss and a whole lot of grace, he was demolishing Brad, pushing him back a step at a time. As she watched, Septimus slashed forward, his face resolute, his expression murderous.

Brad was in big trouble.

"Mommy, he's not going to kill Daddy, is he?" Tuesday asked doubtfully.

Kally woke up. No matter how good he was at it, Septimus was not going to promote armed violence in front of her child. She stepped forward, waving her arms, angry enough to put herself in the line of fire. "Stop this right now!" she called out. "I am not standing for this, do you hear me?"

With a look of extreme surprise, Septimus stopped in his tracks and dropped his blade. "Kally?"

It was only a momentary lapse, but it was enough time for Brad to let out a horrifying yell and knock him over the head with his weapon.

Kally gasped as Septimus went down in a heap.

Brad crowed, "Okay, that's it. I win. Now you have to get out of town, knight boy!"

Kally didn't care what the hell these imbeciles had agreed to. As she ran to Septimus, she shouted at Brad, "This is *my* life you're talking about, not some stupid bet. I don't care what you do or say or threaten, Brad. You are irrelevant. And you didn't even fight fair, you jerk!"

"Kally, I—" he started, but she pushed past him.

Cradling Septimus in her arms, she whispered fiercely, "You're not going anywhere."

"But your apartment—your job—Tuesday," he protested. "You could lose them all because of me."

She kissed his forehead, brushing wet tendrils of hair back, holding him as tight as she could. "I'm not losing anything," she assured him. "Least of all you."

Dragging her purse around, she managed to pull out her gift.

"It's a green card," she said proudly. "You're official. Look—Septimus Sparrow, born in Caernavon, Wales, May 10, 1968. I remembered the book said you were born on a misty morning in May. So I picked a date for you. Is it okay?"

"It's perfect." And, as the people nearby cheered, Tuesday the loudest of all, Septimus framed her face with his hands and kissed her quite thoroughly.

"Hey, wait a minute," Brad argued, "we had a deal—"

He didn't get to finish his sentence, however. Out of nowhere, a huge white horse came galloping up, carrying a massive knight in shiny gold armor. With a flourish, Crispin swung himself off the horse and held up his sword.

"My comrade has fallen," he declared, in his best ringing tones. "I shall answer for him. You shall see this day who reigns as the finest knight in Christendom."

A larger crowd began to gather as Crispin knocked Brad off his feet with his first thrust. It wasn't much of a fight, although the spectators seemed to enjoy the display. The Golden Knight had finished soundly thrashing Brad when the authorities and Lindy Dale, the redheaded reporter, all arrived in a rush.

The police pulled Crispin away from his vanquished foe, announcing something about armor stolen from the Metropolitan Museum of Art. It seemed Cris had some explaining to do.

"You created identification for me," Septimus

noted from his spot on the sidelines. "What about Sir Crispin?"

"He can fend for himself," Kally replied absently. She peered into the crowd behind Lindy Dale and her camera crew. For a second, she could have sworn she saw Mr. Kew, the little old man from the bookshop, in his distinctive headgear, but then he disappeared.

Kally smiled, drawing her daughter into the charmed circle of her embrace with Septimus. "I can only worry about one knight at a time."

Epilogue

"Oh, brother." Kally tossed the *TV Guide* facedown on the floor. One more magazine with Crispin's face on it, and she was going to start a bonfire.

This one said "TV's Hunk du Jour," with a picture of Cris, all hair and teeth and pectoral muscles, holding a sword over his head. She'd felt pretty sure he would land on his feet even after the mess with the museum, and *that* he had definitely done. As the "hunk du jour," he was starring in a syndicated sword-and-sorcery show, and his face was plastered over everything from a shampoo ad to the cover of *People.*

Lindy Dale, the redhead from Channel KBAC, was apparently along for the ride—she'd up and quit the news to manage his career!

But Kally could hardly begrudge Cris his newfound fame. After all, he was perfect for it. And it kept him far, far away from her life, which was even better.

"Mommy, did I show you today's pages?" Tuesday asked from the window seat in their sunny, beautiful new apartment.

Tuesday had been bound and determined to recreate

her favorite book—the one that had started out as *Sir Crispin, the Golden Knight of Yore*—ever since it disappeared while they were all at the fair. That had been months ago, of course, and even though she was making progress, it wasn't much of a book yet.

But in her heart, Kally wasn't sorry to see that book go. It was a record of Septimus's other life, and she might have been interested to hold on to it for that. And she was genuinely sorry its gorgeous watercolor illustrations were lost to the world. But otherwise—well, that book had been kind of scary.

"No, I haven't seen today's pages. Come show me, sweet pea," she said happily, ready to give her daughter a big squeeze. Dutifully, she cast an eye on her daughter's work. "But, Tues, that's not what the other book was like. This one is much..." She wanted to say *better*.

"Uh-huh, I know. Tim and me decided to change it."

"Oh, you did, did you?" Kally asked.

As if he'd heard his name mentioned, Septimus strolled in from the kitchen, where he was experimenting with a wok and a new cookbook. "My egg rolls are terrible," he grumbled.

"But your book is wonderful," Kally told him.

He ambled nearer, bending to kiss her cheek. "And so is my wife. Do you like my book, Mrs. Sparrow?"

"I do indeed, Mr. Sparrow." She looped her arms around him and kissed him, wondering how long Tuesday would be at her ballet lesson and if they had time for a little...

"We don't," he whispered, reading her mind. "Besides, I'm working on my book."

"Our book," Tuesday chimed in.

"Our book," he agreed, ruffling her hair, making her squeal. "I'm thinking of sending this in to an agent. After all, now that I'm training Mel Gibson's stunt double, I've got connections."

Kally bit back a smile. Brad had been furious, but it was true. After his beautiful fighting style was observed on the field at the fair, Septimus had become one of New York's most in-demand stage combat trainers. And because he loved Tuesday, he'd helped her irresponsible father get work. Nothing exciting, of course. That would always be beyond Brad. But at least he was working.

"So what do you think?" Septimus continued. "I'm thinking it can be a series of fantasy novels, all about this dark, mysterious knight and his many adventures."

"Sir Septimus, the Magical Knight of Yore," Kally read off the top of the page. Like everything else in her life, it was... "Perfect."

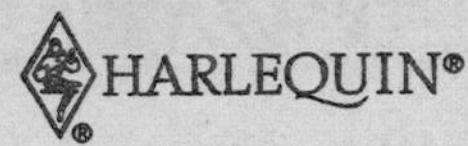

Not The Same Old Story!

Exciting, glamorous romance stories that take readers around the world.

Sparkling, fresh and tender love stories that bring you pure romance.

Bold and adventurous—Temptation is strong women, bad boys, great sex!

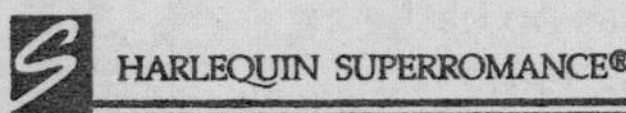

Provocative and realistic stories that celebrate life and love.

Contemporary fairy tales—where anything is possible and where dreams come true.

Heart-stopping, suspenseful adventures that combine the best of romance and mystery.

Humorous and romantic stories that capture the lighter side of love.

Look us up on-line at: http://www.romance.net HGENERIC

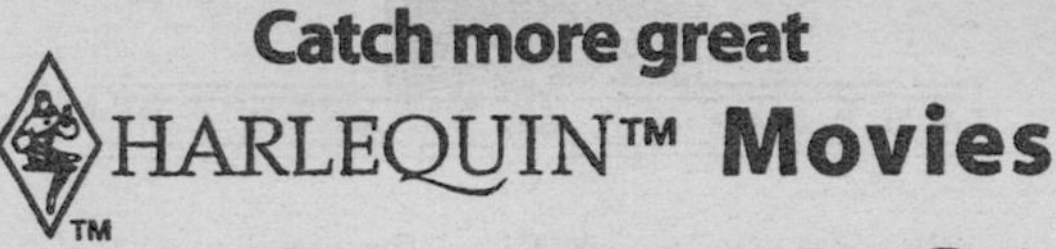

featured on the movie channel tmc

Premiering August 8th

The Waiting Game

Based on the novel by *New York Times* bestselling author Jayne Ann Krentz

Don't miss next month's movie!
Premiering September 12th
A Change of Place
Starring Rick Springfield and Stephanie Beacham. Based on the novel by bestselling author Tracy Sinclair

If you are not currently a subscriber to The Movie Channel, simply call your local cable or satellite provider for more details. Call today, and don't miss out on the romance!

100% pure movies.
100% pure fun.

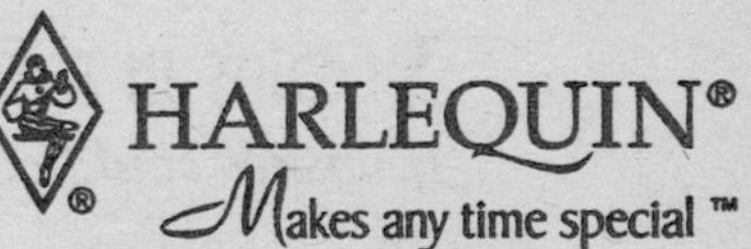

An Alliance Television Production

PHMBPA898